Ladlass

This book belongs to:
Nuala Good
Tandragee - 840273

Ladlass

Bette Paul

André Deutsch Children's Books

First published in 1991 by
André Deutsch Children's Books
an imprint of
Scholastic Publications Limited
7-9 Pratt Street, London NW1 0AE

Copyright © 1991 by Bette Paul
All rights reserved

ISBN 0 233 98710 X paperback
ISBN 0 233 98749 5 hardback

Typeset by AKM Associates (UK) Ltd,
Ajmal House, Hayes Road, Southall, London
Printed in Great Britain by
WBC Bridgend

Chapter 1

"There's a splendid view from the top!" That was the Geography tutor, Mr Baxter – Soupy to us. I could tell from his voice that there wouldn't be a view; it was all jolly, and encouraging and . . . nervy. I mean, there would be a view on the right sort of day, but you didn't have to be a meteorological genius to know that this was not one of them. Poor old Soupy, I thought. Although he wasn't old, really.

I bent my back, pulled on my cagoule strings in a pathetic attempt at keeping the rain out and pushed onwards – and upwards. "Mist," he called it. "We're at cloud level," he'd chortled just as we stepped into a sodden – sodding – white wall of nothing. When does condensation become precipitation? It wasn't mist that was seeping down my back, it was bloody rain. My sympathy for Soupy evaporated.

We all followed Soupy up this track, deep between two very wet dry-stone walls. Why two, I wondered. It was daft enough to build even one wall right up there on the fell. I let the others go and paused to get my breath, propping myself on a big oblong stone that looked as if it had been a gatepost. What for? Who would need to be shut in – or out of – that god-forsaken hole?

As if in reply to my ponderings, the last group of lads overtook me.

"Come over faint, have yer?"

"Giving up, then, are you?"

"Poor little thing – want to go home to your mam?"

They ended their witty chorus with a loud jeer and disappeared into the rain – sorry – mist, yowling, "You'll never walk aloooone." I had no intention of being left to walk alone in that fog, on that fell, in all my sodding clobber. I could just see three of them stepping daintily from stone to stone like puppets dancing. I squelched on, feeling mud ease its way through the lace-holes in my fell-boots. I didn't care. God knows I'd had enough time to get used to it by then; it had rained all and every day since we'd come to the Tarn House to do course work for Geog or Biology A-level.

Course work? Oh yeah, of course. Traipsing around in the siling rain, catching pneumonia, that'd get me an A-Level Geog all right. The rain – sorry – the mist – dropped off my glasses, off my nose-end, off my chin. Seeing nothing I missed a squelch and slithered down onto a rock.

"Sodding hell!"

"Hurt yourself, Roslyn?" Soupy Baxter was right over me.

I staggered up. God! Even my knickers were soaked now.

"The name's Lyn," I muttered.

And that's the least of my troubles. I mean, I don't rate Roslyn at all; reminds me of baby powder, pink frills and lace nighties. But it can be cut to a neat little word – monosyllable, my English teacher calls it. It still sounds soft and soppy but if you just mutter it nearly disappears. Not like our surname. Wait for it – Bugge. Can you believe it? Why my Grandad or my Dad didn't get round to changing it I don't know. I can only think they want every new generation of our family to suffer as they did. Roslyn Bugge, that's me. The nicknames I leave to you, but don't kid yourself they're original – or funny.

"Ach, come on then, Lyn," said Soupy, giving me a hand up. I was so surprised I took it and let him pull me along to the top. It did seem funny, to be walking hand in hand with a teacher, but I had to admit, I needed that lift up.

And he was very nice about it, not chatting or urging me along, just plodding silently, guiding me out of the worst of the mud and smiling a bit now and then. For a moment it felt as if there was only us two in all that quiet space. For a moment I was nearly happy. It was a short moment though.

"Aye, aye. Where've you been, sir? In the heather with Livid Lyn?"

"Be careful, sir, she bites does that one – not in interesting places either."

"What're you doing with that ladlass, Mr Baxter, when there's lovely girls like us around?"

And so on and so forth, banter, banter, banter. Right suave lot that Geog set. They made me sick. Them and everybody else at that college. Soupy walked me straight through them and told everybody to follow on. I felt a right fool, leading the group. But Soupy kept me walking with him along the track until we reached a sort of stone hut. He unlocked the big wooden door and led us all in.

It was just one room with a stone floor and a few benches. There was only a window at one end, and when the last one shut the door, it was nearly dark. So of course the boys had to start whooo-ing and howling in a spooky way. The girls cooperated by squealing so I had a chance to bag a bench, take off my rucksack and sit.

God, I was knackered! Funny, I was full of energy some days and dead tired on others. I just sat, listening to the daft noises from the others, too tired even to get my packed lunch out. I peered at the blurred images across the room. My glasses must need cleaning, I thought, but I couldn't be bothered.

"Hey, are you all right?" I didn't know the girl who sat on my bench. She wasn't in my group else she wouldn't have sat with me.

I nodded and shut my eyes. I could have slept right there on that hard bench, but this lass kept twitting on. She took a packet out of her rucksack and slammed it on the side of the bench to break it. Then she offered me some; it gleamed ever so white in the dim light. But I shook my head. I was too tired to eat. Besides, my mouth was really dry; that was ironic, considering how wet I was outside.

"Eat!" she ordered, pushing the stuff at me. "You need something for energy. Everest climbers eat this, so it's good enough for us."

She bit a chunk off the bar and crunched it loudly. She didn't seem to be lacking energy. I pushed my piece into my mouth and sucked on it. It was very sweet, and very minty.

"Kendal mint-cake," she explained through a mouthful. "Chew it up and have another. It quenches your thirst and raises your energy-level."

"Does it dry wet jeans?" I asked, sarcastically.

She laughed in a low, gurgly way, not shrieking like the others. "There you are, you see," she said. "You're feeling better already. Have some more."

She was right, I was feeling better. I pulled my hood off and shook my damp head. My short fuzzy hair clung to my head, soaked with the sweat inside the hood.

"Now eat your lunch," she ordered. "It'll drive the mint-cake round faster."

I nearly laughed, but I was still too wet and tired. "You sound like my grandma, ordering everybody about," I said.

"Your grandma probably knows more about survival in these conditions than I do. But I have studied metabolic rates."

We unwrapped the cling-film from our baps and chewed silently. The others were still larking about, flipping bits of crust at each other and squirting fizzy coke. I noticed they were coming back into focus now.

"What was that about metals, you said you studied?" I asked after two cheese rolls and a Penguin. "At least I feel alive again, now."

"That's exactly it. Your metabolism is balanced again now, your energy level is up. Metabolism is the rate at which we convert our food into energy. I bet you didn't have much breakfast this morning."

"I had a cup of tea and some toast," I said.

"And then set out on a ten-mile hike over rough country in foul weather. Yes. Well, no wonder."

She was a strange lass, talking like an old granny, or a doctor, looking like a schoolgirl with her pale smooth face and lengths of fairish hair plastered on her forehead. She told me she was taking maths and sciences and the Geog was just an extra.

"Insurance," she explained. "Just in case."

"In case what?"

"In case I don't make it to medical school."

"Well, thanks for the consultation," I said. "The treatment seems to have worked. If you need a reference for that medical school, I'll write you one."

She laughed and passed me another block of the miracle mint-cake. "Keep it in your pocket for this afternoon's stint. And don't let yourself get that low again this week. Eat a lot more than you do at home. It's a tough life out here."

I saw Anna a few times at the Study Centre, but she was

usually with a group of lads we called 'boffs' – meaning clever, scientific students. I wasn't part of that crowd – or any other crowd, come to think of it. Soupy was always on at me to join the others, but I knew they didn't want me. I don't know what was the worst part of that week: the days of trudging around in the rain or the evenings of jolly games. In between, we had to work on a diary and sketch-book of the day's expeditions and cook the supper. I hated cookery at school, fiddling around cutting radishes into water-lilies and beating hell out of cake mixture, but at the Field Centre you only had to open the freezer and a few tins and there was supper for twenty. Any idiot could do it – I could do it. In fact I often swapped duties with the others so that I could cook and miss the homework, then wash-up and miss the jollifications.

I sometimes wondered what our Mam would have said if she could have seen me slaving away in the kitchen. At home Kev and me had arguments about washing up – and usually we both won. Dad couldn't stand the noise so he washed the pots. If he could see me now, I thought, it'd bring tears to his eyes. But these days everything did. Mam would have turned me out of the kitchen into the classroom, but I was just too fagged by the end of the day to do anything intelligent. During the walks, when we were supposed to be collecting data for the homework, I was propping myself up somewhere, trying to get the energy for the next hike. It didn't seem fair, puffing and panting at the tail end of the twenty-a-day lads when I never ever smoked. I never ever realised I was so unfit, either.

I found out, though, on the last day when we had to take maps and compasses and find our own way back. Soupy took us out in the mini-bus, gave us a list of clues that we had to follow and left us to it. It was actually fine, too, but grey and cold. I couldn't use a compass so I tagged on to Anna's group. They were all boffs who were doing top A-Level sciences. They were also very tall, even the girls. I had to work three times as hard as they did just to keep up.

"We have to head down the valley after this turn," somebody called from the front.

"No we don't, we can get back over the tops," said Gary Baldwin.

"I know we can get back over the tops, you nerk. That's not the point; we've got to follow Soupy's route to pick up the answers to his clues."

"No we haven't. We've got to stop playing silly buggers, get the worst of the walk over, then stop in the pub for the rest of the afternoon."

This argument went on while we walked along the road. Even I could hear it from fifty yards back. I saw them all stop by some steps in the stone wall; some set off down to the valley road but a few lads were climbing the steps when I caught up. "What're you doing?" I puffed.

"Oh God, it's Ladlass Lyn!"

"Piss off, this is a stag party."

"She thinks that's where she belongs. Macho Maiden!"

Gary Baldwin lived near us; he had been in my gang when we were kids. He pointed down the road. "The right route is down there – follow the boffs. We're taking a short-cut on our own."

I nodded. I was used to this. Without speaking, I set off down the road after the others. Even if they were well ahead, the road was better than that vertical hillside.

"You OK, Lyn?" Gary shouted from the top of the wall.

I didn't turn, just jerked my thumb up. What the hell would he do if I wasn't?

By now I'd lost sight of both parties but that didn't bother me; I'd got used to being on my own now. It had been different when I was a kid; I was always out on the streets with my gang, building dens, climbing walls, racing bikes across the allotments. I'd always been a leader until we went up to the comprehensive. After that the gangs seemed to melt away. The same lads were there, but they played different games: team games like football or cricket, with rules that excluded girls. The girls went to aerobics, gymnastics or dancing classes. I took to staying in and scribbling. I even got to like being on my own; at least that's what I always said when our Kev offered to take me out.

On my own right now didn't feel so great. Surely I had put on enough speed to meet the others? I felt puffed enough anyway. The road dropped into the village and I stopped to get my breath, and my lunch-time apple.

I went to the nearest wall and leant against the bus stop. At home I often didn't eat anything until dinner and I never even noticed. It must be all this exercise and fresh air that was killing me. Wait till I saw Dad. Do me good indeed! I might even raise a smile when I told him. Just.

Chewing hard, I looked at the map, framed in a plastic holder, tied round my neck. I could see the road I'd just walked along, and find the track across the hills that the lads had taken, and – that was it – the footpath along the dale, just before the dip into the village, where the boffs had gone. I'd been so far away in the past that I'd missed it.

"One of these days you'll be in real trouble with that dreaming of yours," our Mam told me, very regularly. And now I was.

I set off up the hill, feeling sick. After the apple my energy should improve, according to Dr Anna-Boff-Hitchens. The thought of Anna cheered me up a bit: if I could catch them up, she might talk to me a bit. I moved back out of the village, my legs feeling as if they were under water, found the track and turned off the road onto the soft wet grass of the dale.

Chapter 2

I started off quite cheerful – for me.

"Why don't you smile sometimes, our Lyn? It might make you look attractive," our Mam said almost daily. "No wonder you've got no friends; you're hardly the life and soul of the party, are you?"

Well, I wasn't, but left to myself I might be the life and soul of my own party. Why did everybody keep on at me about friends? I could do without. I'm a lot happier with my scribbles than giggling with the girls or grappling with the boys of a Saturday night.

It was a Saturday morning when all this field-study-lark started. Dad had been tidying up – again – and found my letter from college. When I went down to the kitchen he was poring over it.

"Field studies . . . Tarn House. . . November. . . ." Dad was blinking as he read it out to Kev.

"Eeh bah gum, fancy sending them college kids to study out in fields! We all know what they'll be studying out there." Kev was doing his impersonation of a professional

Yorkshireman. "Ah never knew there was sustificates for that."

"If there was you'd never get one," I told him. I can be quite withering at times.

"'Ark at the sex-pot of South Yorks!" he jeered. His stubbly cheeks puffed out as he laughed and his bright blue piggy eyes twinkled. He's four years older than me but not much bigger. He's got such ridiculous long golden curls that he looks like my younger sister. You don't tell him that, of course.

"Eeh, ah don't know about this," said Dad. He wasn't doing an impersonation, he just talks like that. "Ah don't know, I'm sure." And he's not; he's never sure of anything these days. "It'll cost, you know, and your mam's got enough on." He was right there. Our Mam had the lot of us on: Dad signing on sick, Kev signing on the social, and me not even signing. Then she had her job on the Housing Association, her place on the Council, her fund-raising for the homeless, her dozens of meetings. No wonder Dad . . .

"Never mind," I said quicckly, to stop him getting his shakes. "I don't want to go." I did, though. For one thing, I'd already capped two humanities outings to Stratford because they were so expensive. If I missed this one I'd be in trouble.

"Nay, you should go if it's for college. And you'll enjoy it right up there. It'll be like we used to . . ." Dad was off again, his eyes filled with tears. Kev looked across the table at me and raised his eyebrows. I scowled back. Our Kev and Dad represent the two unacceptable faces of unemployment: the one won't work for a living and the other can't live without working. They should do a documentary about them.

As usual, as I knew all along he would, he copped out. "It'll be for your mam to decide."

And of course, she did; very decisive, our Mam, especially

when it comes to education. She handed over the money without so much as wincing, though it was the best part of her week's wages. "It'll do you good to get away with a few intelligent young folk," she said. "But think on, I want no skiving. I want you to come back with plenty of work done, with some friends and with a smile. All right?" Trust our Mam to give with one hand and take away with the other.

Well, by this last day, I'd done no real work, made no friends, and I didn't feel at all like smiling. In fact I felt terribly dry suddenly. I looked at the river alongside me; it clattered onwards, clear and dark over the rocks. It looked so cold and clear that I stopped at the edge and wondered whether to drink some.

I bent over the shallow water and suddenly remembered the last time Soupy had dropped back to walk with me. We were following a stream along a flat valley bottom so the going was easy. I was still way behind; I just never seemed to get into my stride that morning, scuttling fast to catch up then lagging behind to get my breath. Soupy met me on a bend in the stream and strode along, matching his steps to mine and smiling down at me now and then. Together we approached the little bridge where the others were gathered.

Gary Baldwin was filling his water bottle at the stream. Soupy had warned us about that but when Gary saw him, he deliberately took a long drink. Soupy just walked on, talking in a clear, carrying voice. He told us about the time he had filled his water-bottle from a peaty stream up in the Highlands, hundreds of miles from any industrial pollution. Soupy drank that water as he wended his way up the hillside, where he discovered the rotting carcase of a sheep straddling the stream. We all laughed at that. Except for Gary, who looked a bit pale.

Now, my stomach heaved at the thought. I was sweating

too, and dizzy with the effort of walking. I stopped and listened. There was the eternal, infernal sound of running water and nothing else. Surely I should have caught up with the boffs by now? I felt as though I had walked for hours, but my watch was back in my locker and the day was so grey I couldn't tell whether it was past noon.

I leaned against a great outcrop, breathing fast, trying to keep down the feeling of sickness. I felt something hard in my cagoule pocket – the remains of the mint-cake Anna Hitchens had given me the other day. I crunched it slowly, remembering the friendly boff's advice about metabolism.

That's what was making me feel so rotten, I thought, pressing onwards upstream. What I needed was a good dinner.

"What you need is a good dinner inside you," my gran said every Sunday when she came to us. "Get some flesh on them bones. All this dieting nonsense." It was no use protesting that I didn't diet because Gran never listened to anything, unless it was on television.

"You'll go and catch that disease," she said, with satisfaction. She seemed to like the idea of me catching a disease.

"What disease?" I asked her.

"That anoraks disease you lasses all get."

Kev bust a gut laughing. "You hear that, Lyn? Your old anorak looks as if it's got a disease to pass on to you. I should gèt a new one if I was you." And he laughed all over his Yorkshire pudding and gravy.

"Anorexia, Clara," our Mam corrected her.

"Aye well, be that as it may. That's what she's got, all skin and bone. You mun' feed her up. Give her some dumplings and some suet puddings."

Ugh! There's this belief in Yorkshire that you have to be 'bonny' — meaning big and hefty. Lots of the women of our

Mam's age are hefty and muscular – size twenty upwards; even at school there were plenty of girls who weighed twelve stone and more. I'm short, like my dad, and skinny, like our Mam. And not over fond of stodge: steamed pudding and custard I can do without, and as for the fried breakfasts my dad used to demand, in his bread-winning days, well, the very smell of sizzling bacon of a morning made me heave.

A great wave of sickness rose in me now. I turned off the path, put my head into a bramble bush and retched . . . and retched . . . and . . .

There was the most disgusting smell. I had to get away from that bush. I couldn't believe that I had made that stench; somebody must have dumped some chemical there. It was a chemical sort of smell, like gallons of nail-varnish remover.

Without consulting my map I pressed upwards away from the water. Now I was so faint and so sweaty that I didn't care which route I took, so long as it led back. I was climbing up on my hands and knees, the top of the dale swirling above me. I thought if I made it right to the top, I would have a clear view of the track to Tarn House.

Gasping and grasping at ferns and brambles and grasses, I pulled myself upwards. When I reached the top, I rolled over the edge and lay wallowing in sweat and sick and tears.

Amazingly, I must have slept. When I woke up it was darker than ever and I was parched. Not just thirsty, but dried out; my mouth had no spit in it at all, and my tongue was thick and rough. I had to get some water, even before I set off again. I sat up, holding onto the earth to stop it shifting around me; then I risked standing. There was a stony track along the ridge so I turned back along it towards the sound of rushing water. Reeling like a drunken yobbo I followed the noise.

It was a waterfall; gallons and gallons of clear water

tumbling down the hillside into a deep gorge. I just had to risk drinking some of it. It ought to be clean, this far up the dale. And anyway I knew I couldn't go on without it. The sweating must have dried me out. I stepped off the track towards the gushing, clattering, gurgling water, plunged my head under it and sucked great globs of living, writhing water down, down, down.

And that's the last I remember about Wanseldale.

Chapter 3

I remembered it well-enough later, when all the questions started, all the statements were made.

Apparently, Soupy came out to check up on us. He hoiked Gary and the lads out of the pub and set them back on the test route – hours late. I smiled when I heard that; I could just imagine him lifting one very black eyebrow and calmly suggesting that they should make a start on the day's work. Trust Soupy to make the punishment fit the crime.

It seems that he then drove round the top road, where he got a glimpse of the boffs making slow progress, with maps and cameras and note-books at the ready. He assumed I was with them because Gary had told him I was and because they were going quite slow enough even for me.

So, having caught the Skivers and checked on the Boffs, he went to the pub with the field-centre warden for dinner and a pint. And why not? He'd worked damned hard all week with us; he deserved a break.

Still, as was noted later, many, many times, he didn't do a

head-count, did he? Well no, but we weren't primary school kids, were we?

According to the warden's statement, they were in the pub an hour, then they took the mini-bus back to Tarn House and awaited results. First home was – guess who? Yes, of course, Gary Baldwin and his mates. Of course they'd ignored all the clues and orienteering on the way, but they'd done the whole route at a fair trot. Soupy calmly screwed up their un-answer papers and set them on cooking.

It was dark when the Boffs turned up, clutching reams of paper and looking, according to Gary, "shagged out". In all the fuss of checking their answers and arguing over a mis-printed grid-reference, nobody missed me. Well, they wouldn't, would they? They went off to shower and if the other three girls had even given me a thought, which they wouldn't, they'd have assumed I was in my usual place in the kitchen.

As it was the end of the course, Soupy had hired a (strictly non-educational) video, the others organised a bit of a disco, with Gary's ghetto-blaster, and they were all set to enjoy a final fling. But before all that, there was the cleaning rota to organise for next morning. Most teachers would have made a list and stuck it on the notice board, but Soupy liked folk to work things out for themselves. Democracy, I think they call it.

It was during the heated arguments that I was missed.

Soupy went down the list, matching names with duties.

". . . ten, eleven, twelve . . .? Where's Lyn?"

Anna told me of the total silence at that moment.

Gary told me they all started arguing about who had seen me last.

They both mentioned Soupy's white face.

The warden organised the search party.

*

It was the dog that got me. I could feel hot breath panting down my neck. Not given to sexual fantasies (all right then, not given to admitting to them), I thought of Komrad and pushed it away.

Komrad was the family dog when I was little. Dad had brought him home from the foundry, Grandad had trained him, Kev had given him a name and our Mam, in spite of all her moaning, fed him. Komrad lived either with us or at Grandad's; he slept wherever he happened to end up, but when he was back home with us, he always came up to lick me awake. As he seemed to be doing now.

"Whaaa . . .?" I could just open my eyes; not that it did me any good – it was pitch-dark. "Geroff, Komrad." I pushed out with an arm and turned back to snuggle into the quilt. But there wasn't a quilt. There wasn't a bed. There wasn't a Komrad; he had died soon after Grandad. I know I thought all these thoughts, but they didn't seem to matter. I didn't think "Where am I?" like they do in books. I didn't even care. If only the passionate animal would get off my back I could go back to my deep, deep sleep.

Well, he didn't. He whined and barked and led the rescue team up the path to the falls.

I came round in the ambulance. I had drips in both arms and cooking foil all over me. The first person I saw was Soupy. He looked terrible.

"You look terrible, sir," I croaked. Soupy's bright blue eyes widened and he squeezed my hand so hard it hurt. He didn't speak, just kept on looking right at me, into me.

"Can I have a drink, sir?" I whispered.

An officious uniform leaned over and dripped about three drops of water into my dried-up mouth. It was cruel – I needed a gallon to quench my thirst.

"Och, Lyn, how're you feeling noo?" asked Soupy. His

voice was husky, as if he'd used it all up. As indeed he had, shouting across the moors.

"Dry – more water."

"Not now, young lady. You can only have enough to moisten your lips as yet." The officious uniform spoke. "Rest quiet now."

I wanted to protest, to grumble, but I had no words. You know how people say "words fail me" and then go on to lambast you with about two hundred? Well, just then, words really did fail me; I couldn't find them anywhere. So I just looked at Soupy and wondered what had happened to make him look so poorly.

He kept on looking at me and dabbing my face with a cool damp cloth. Like Gran used to when we had 'flu. It was so comforting that I tried to smile.

If only Mam could see me, actually smiling!

But there was no Mam. It was Dad who met us at the hospital. I was quite gobsmacked. I hadn't seen Dad outside the house for nearly a year. I tried to sit up to talk to him, but my arms had no strength. He leaned over the trolley, fringed with dangling drips bottles and looking frightened.

"Your mum's in a meeting," he said, as if to explain his visit.

Well she would be, wouldn't she?

I just nodded. That was all I could do. I travelled along a corridor so bright that the light hurt my eyelids. With Dad running along one side of me and Soupy the other, I felt as if I was taking part in one of those John O'Groats to Land's End pram races.

Then I was whisked off into a cubicle, away from them both. Thank God!

"Has anyone ever told you you have diabetes mellitus?"

It was the next day when I heard the words for the first time.

"What?"

"You're a diabetic."

"I am not. I'm perfectly fit – I'm not even fat."

"That has nothing to do with your case," the woman told me. I had no idea who she was; that's the trouble with institutions, you never know who you're talking to. She was dressed like an old-fashioned school teacher – you know, grey flannel suit, crisp shirt, grey tights and good court-shoes.

Suddenly the tide of frustration which had been rising all morning, as they refused to let my parents in, refused to let me get to the phone, the shower, even the lavatory, rose up and burst through the banks of exhaustion.

"I've not got diabetes emmy-what-not. I've been suffering from exhaustion and exposure and am now rested and well. I am ready to go home." I didn't quite yell at her; I wasn't brave enough to.

"You won't be going home for a while yet. You'll be staying under observation until you're balanced." She got up, as if to leave.

"I'm balanced enough as it is. I don't need to be observed. I just want to get home."

Funny, that. The way you hate home and long to get away from it most of the time; but as soon as somebody tells you you can't, it becomes the most desirable place on earth.

"Get me out of here. Take these things off me!" I was yelling now, and pulling at the drip tubes which still attached me to the hanging bottles.

The woman did not turn one elegant grey hair. "Yes," she agreed, very quietly. "We are just going to do that."

That shut me up.

A man in a white jacket came over and unscrewed the

tubes. Then he took out the needles from my heels and my wrists, very gently. Even so, they were long needles and I shuddered as he collected them from my flesh.

"Never you mind, luv, you'll soon be used to them things; they'll be your life-line," he joked – didn't he? as he wheeled the gadgetry away.

"There you are, one step at a time," said the teacherish woman. "I'm Dr Ransome and I'm going to help you get back home, and back to normal."

"When?"

"That depends on you. If you are intelligent, cooperative and disciplined, it could take a week or ten days." Christ, she sounded worse than any school teacher.

"But I'm better now."

"Yes you are," she agreed. "But only because of the insulin drip. It won't last."

"What do you mean?"

She licked her glossy lips. Under the glasses and the severe hair, she was really good-looking. She shoved her hair back with a thin, young-looking hand. "You have a malfunction which we call diabetes mellitus – sugar diabetes, if you prefer."

"The only thing I prefer is to be out of this place."

"Yes, well, you will be. But not until we have taught you how to live with your condition."

"What condition? I don't believe you, I haven't got a condition. I was worn out on that damned field course, but I'm better now. I just won't go on any field courses again, that's all. Who cares?"

She was very cool. I wanted to kick and scream, to hurl my pillow – even my bed at her. I clenched my fists and beat on the blanket. But she only muttered "Irritability . . . typical at this stage . . . new blood test." She swept through the floral curtains and left me alone in my prison – sorry – cubicle.

I leaned on my pillow holding my breath. If I let go, I thought, I would wreck the place. I felt so angry and so strong, when a wave of fury swept over me I grabbed my sheet and pulled it between both fists.

There was a terrible sound of ripping linen.

I looked down, horrified. I was enough of my mother's daughter to value good bedding. And I'd destroyed a sheet. Suddenly I felt so ashamed – and so weak. I just held on to the two strips of the sheet and put my head down and wept. Silently, in case there was anyone around.

And that was the beginning of my education.

Over the next three days I learned a lot, fast.

I learned how to test my urine with colour-coded strips, then how to read the results. I learned how to prick my thumb to take blood, drip the blood onto another strip, count thirty seconds, and then interpret that result. And, of course, I learned how to give myself an insulin injection. All that in three days. I was very determined to get out.

"You'll be getting out of here in record time," chirped one of the nurses, supervising my injection. "Once you can manage without closing your eyes, that is," she added bitchily. I was still squeamish about the injection.

"You'll be back at college in no time," announced our Mam, when she managed to fit in a visit to me between committee meetings at the Town Hall.

Note: she did not say "back home". Back to college was more important to her than being at home.

To be fair – and where my mother's concerned I am not – she did arrive as soon as they'd given me a new sheet and told me to remake the bed.

"What's this then?" she asked. "Results of more

government cuts? Shall I go down the chippie and get your supper?" Trust my mother to turn even an illness into political capital.

"No – you can't. It seems that I'll be on a permanent and boring diet for the rest of my life." I flounced back into bed and made a fuss of puffing up my pillows.

"Nay, it's not that bad," she said, without a trace of sympathy in her voice. "My mother had diabetes for years."

"And look what it did to her," I glowered.

"What do you mean? She was seventy-six and feeling fine when she got run over. If it hadn't been for that idiot driver she'd be here today."

"I didn't mean that. I meant . . . well . . . the sort of person she was."

"Just what sort of person was she?"

"Well, you said yourself often enough."

"Yes, but what do you say?"

Suddenly I felt tired. I wasn't ready for that battle yet.

"Oh. never mind," I muttered, leaning back on my pillows, hoping I looked pale, if not interesting.

"I do mind. I mind that my mother was a down-trodden, depressing and boring sort of person, but she had plenty to be depressed about; you haven't." She paused, to let that sink in. "And I must say, Lyn, you do seem to have inherited her temperament as well as her diabetes." You can hear why my mam does so well on committees, can't you?

I looked across at her, through drooping eyelids. There she sat, upright in the hard chair, looking as if she was set for the day, though we both knew she had better things to do. She looked a bit more faded than usual; a bit more her age. Often she looked about thirty, with her smooth oily complexion, her shining brown eyes and her thick bobbed hair. Good bones, good teeth, wide mouth – even without makeup she was attractive. I didn't take after her. I was all wild fuzz and freckles like Grandma – the dead one. I yawned and sighed.

"I know you want me to go, Roslyn, but I think we ought to talk about it." And even before she went on I mouthed her favourite words with her: "You must face up to things."

That's what she loved doing, facing up to things. If there were no things to be faced up to, she'd go out and find some.

"Mu-u-um. Just leave me alone for a bit. Eh?" I didn't often plead with her, but I was feeling weak and weepy again. I opened my eyes and looked at her, standing now, all five feet of her, leaning over the bed. There was a deep line each side of her mouth, and her eyes looked cloudy.

"Yes, well, I'll let you rest, then. Kev's coming later, and then your dad tonight. See you soon, Lyn."

She bent over and kissed me; I could smell her musky perfume, feel her finger tips on my forehead. I wanted to throw myself across the bed and beg her to take me back home, to put the clock back and make me whole again. I wanted her to cuddle me and soothe me like those mother-earth women in foreign films. I wanted to hear her whisper consolations in an exotic language. Tears were still oozing down my face (what a wally! what a wimp!) as I fell asleep.

Chapter 4

A clattering noise woke me up: Gran, bashing away at the pots again.

"Gran?" I inquired. But the figure by my bed, clearing the top of the locker, was too tall and fair to be our gran. And anyway it was in a pastel nylon overall; definitely not Gran's style.

"Sorry to wake you. Just putting this plant on your locker."

For a moment I smelt wet jeans and felt my glasses steam over.

"Anna Hitchens?" I asked. "Have you brought the mint-cake?"

She laughed that gurgling, quiet laugh that seemed to invite you to join in. "Sorry, we all thought a potted plant would be more suitable; mint-cake's off as far as you're concerned now."

"Everything's off as far as I'm concerned," I grumbled.

"Nonsense. Have a glass of Lucozade and stop feeling so

sorry for yourself." She poured the drink and handed it to me as if she ran the place.

"You still sound like my grandma," I told her, taking the glass. I drank the stuff like a lager-lout on his first pint; I still had a perpetual thirst. "What are you doing here anyway?"

"I came to see you."

"What, all the way across the City?" The hospital was miles out the other side from college. "Just to see me?" I couldn't believe it.

"Well, I was deputed to bear the customary SU offering of vegetation. But I had to come, anyway; I have a part-time job here."

I might have guessed, of course. Isn't it marvellous the way success attracts success? I mean, there was my family, with two unemployed men in it, and here was this bit of a schoolgirl, studying four A-levels and holding down a part-time job in a hospital. No supermarket shelving for Miss Hitchens.

"What do you do?" I asked, knowing it was bound to be something interesting and well-paid; a fascinating little job in a lab, offered by a friend of Daddy's.

"I clean."

"Clean?" I couldn't believe it. "Clean what?"

"Corridors, wards, sluice-rooms – whatever."

"But you're going to be a doctor," I protested.

"Not for many expensive years yet. I need a healthy bank-balance. And any hospital experience is useful. I might turn out to be the only junior doctor who knows how to mend the electric polisher." Anna laughed again. "So how are you?" she asked, with real interest, not sloppy sympathy.

"Och, she's as weell as can be expected, under the cirrcumstaances." I quoted the accepted jargon in Sister Willis's pinched Scots voice.

Anna's shoulders shook as she giggled silently. "Nonsense, young lady," she suddenly boomed. "You are getting better and better every hour of every day. Think positively!" She was being Mrs Hamilton, the physio.

I flopped about in the bed, helpless with laughter. "God," I gasped, "I haven't laughed so much for years. You should do your own act – like Victoria Wood!"

"Oh no, I'm no good on stage, and I certainly can't write; I've tried. I'm producing the Christmas Revue and we're terribly short of material. Hey, you could help me!"

"That's for the drama bods. I can't do anything like that." I'd never had anything to do with the Students' Union at college. I had quite enough of unions at home.

"Oh yes you can, Lyn. For a start, collect all the funny little remarks and incidents you notice around here."

"Collect?"

"Yes – write them down. Just scribble any bits and pieces in any order. We'll use them in a hospital sketch later."

"But I'm no good at that sort of thing," I protested. It wasn't true; I'd been scribbling since I could hold a pencil, but nobody knew.

"And we are, I suppose. Do you think us Boffs – yes, we know what you call us – are naturally talented actors, singers, dancers?"

"No, but. . . ."

"But you are doing A-level Lit; you got straight As for English in GCSE and I read the poetry you published in the Community Arts paper. It was very accomplished. You must have been writing for years."

So much for my secret; damn and blast my ambitious mother.

"Oh that, it was only because my mother knew the chairman of the Arts Committee." I dismissed my poems –

my very own creations – with a scowl and a wave of my hand. Judas!

"You mean Andy Roberts is corruptible? What does your mother offer him, her Yorkshire puddings?"

The thought of my mother even making Yorkshire puddings, never mind wrapping them up and taking them to the editor of 'Tykes' was hilarious.

"You know nowt about Yorkshires and even less about my mam's terrible cooking, Anna Hitchens."

We were still laughing when my next visitor arrived.

"Hello, hello, hello!" Our Kev never says anything once when three times will make it worse. "What's all this, then? Girl talk?"

'Girl talk'! I could have hit him. "It was human conversation, until you dropped by," I glowered. An hour ago I was longing for a visitor, any visitor, even our Kev. Now he'd turned up just when I didn't want anybody, especially not family. I wanted to keep Anna all to myself. She obviously didn't share the sentiment.

"I'm Anna Hitchens," she said, holding out her hand. "I'm at college with Lyn."

"Hard luck, Anna. I hope there's a few nice fellers like me around to make up for our Sis." He leered over and took her hand. I blushed for him. Our Kev is always at his worst in company.

"Plenty," she assured him, taking in the leather jacket and the snow-washed jeans and the Nike trainers. A walking cliché, is our Kev. "Plenty like you but none to make up for your sister. She's an original." Her mouth was twitching as she turned to me. "Bye, Lyn. See you soon; I'm on again at the weekend. And don't forget the scribble." She nodded to Kev and shot off down the ward.

"Thanks for coming – and for the plant, tell them," I called after her.

"Really classy, some of these nurses," said Kev appreciatively as he watched her progress.

"She's not a nurse, she's a cleaner," I explained.

"A cleaner? Slumming a bit for a bonnie lass like that, isn't she?"

"She needs the money. And she's not a 'bonnie lass'. She's taking four A-levels and she's going to be a doctor."

"Is that why she came to see you? To study a specimen?"

I stared straight ahead. Trust my family to spoil anything. I'd thought Anna had come to see me – as me – as a friend. But Kev might be right. She's the sort of student who sees every situation as exam-fodder; a bit of personal knowledge about diabetes might prove useful in an interview.

"You don't need to stay if you're off anywhere," I said to Kev, in a tired voice. I suddenly wanted to be left alone.

"Nay, I promised Mam I'd stay with you for a bit. She thought you were getting depressed."

"You can see I'm not."

"Aye, well, you were certainly having a good laugh with your friend. Mam'll be pleased to hear you've had a visitor from college."

"Will she? Why?"

"You know she's allus whittling on about you having no friends."

"I know she's always whittling on at me."

"She worries about you a lot, does our Mam."

This was news to me. I thought she was always too busy worrying about feeding the Third World, clearing up pollution, the next council election. The really big issues of life, that's what she liked to tackle, not unemployed sons, redundant husbands, or diabetic daughters.

As if he read my thoughts, Kevin went on earnestly, "She teks a lot on, you know. I mean, there can't be many councillors who have an 'ouse to run and kids to bring up."

"Kevin, you live in a dream world. She does take a lot on – up at the council, but me gran does everything at home – shopping, ironing, cooking – the lot. And you and me are not exactly kids, you know, we don't need any bringing-up; when we did, it was our gran who did it!" I ended on a loud note.

"Shhh. . . our Lyn," said Kevin, blushing and peering round at the interested spectators. "Don't go upsetting yourself again."

He placed a bulging plastic carrier on the bed. "There, you see, she does think about you. She's sent your books."

"What books?"

"Your books – from out your room; your homework books."

"That's typical. She doesn't send me get-well presents – not even a grape! She sends work – to make sure I'll pass my exams. Very thoughtful, very caring," I sneered.

"They won't let us bring food, because of balancing your diet. Pr'aps they could balance your mind while they're at it."

"Perhaps if you hung around long enough they might even find yours."

"Aw, our Lyn, you allus was a bad-tempered bitch."

I glowered but didn't answer.

He sighed. "They told us to bring your work; you can have lessons here, you know. Our Mam went to the college in her dinner-hour to sort it all out with them. She was ever so pleased when she got back."

"I'll bet she was; nothing pleases her more than to pile work on to me."

"No . . . I mean she was pleased with what they had to say about you. 'Very promising' they said you were." Kev beamed across the bed at me. "I haven't seen our Mam so pleased since . . . since . . ." He couldn't find the words so he pointed to the plastic carrier on the bed. "Now get on with that lot, if you don't want to end up like me dad and me."

And he went.

I flopped back on the pillows, turned my back on the ward – the world – and wept. It was the old argument; Kevin had always idolised our Mam and the more she 'took on', the more he seemed to worship her. She was working at the Council and on the Union, while our Dad was working flat out on shifts and overtime; they were hardly at home. Kev never seemed to mind coming in to an empty house, getting his own tea, and settling down in front of the telly to wait for her to get back from some political meeting or other. And when she did turn up, he'd be happy as Larry, trotting about making tea, bringing her slippers, listening to her going on about the Council, the Unions, the Government. The very thought of those cosy little homecomings made my eyelids droop. . .

"Lyn? Are you awake, love?"

I could hear Dad's voice. But why should he be asking if I was awake at home time?

"Lyn – waken up, lass." His voice was urgent this time, almost frightened.

"Dad?" I didn't open my eyes, just put a hand out.

"Aye, it's me, love." He squeezed my hand painfully. That made me open my eyes. It wasn't our house, it wasn't home time from school. It was four o'clock though, and I could hear the clatter of the tea trolleys on the corridor.

Sister Willis came bustling up.

"Come along, Lyn, there's tea in the day-room. You can take your daddy along there, dearie." She hustled me off the bed as if lying there was sinful. I looked questioningly at Dad. He couldn't face company just now. But he couldn't stand up to Sister Willis either. He nodded.

We walked in silence to the day room. There was an urn of

tea and some biscuits on a trolley. Out of habit, I sat down and let Dad bring them over.

"I didn't know whether you were allowed any of these, so I brought a selection," he said, putting a little plate of biscuits down on the table. I sipped my tea, which had far too much milk in it and, of course, no sugar. I shuddered.

"Are you all right, then?" he asked.

"As right as I s'll ever be, I suppose." I shoved the biscuits round the plate and took a Rich Tea.

"Ah'm sure you'll feel better when once they've sorted you out, got you balanced, like."

He sounded different, more brisk, more energetic. Was he actually trying to cheer me up? I looked across the top of my cup at him. Once a big man, he seemed to have shrunk inside his skin over the past couple of years; it hung in folds around his heavy neck, below his ears; even his cheeks seemed to be drawn downwards. It was as if his body knew that its strength was not needed now, and the muscles had given up holding it together. When I was a little girl, he was so strong that I used to stub my toe when he invited me to kick his belly – even if I kept my shoes on. When he laughed at me – he was always laughing then – his bright eyes, with baby-pink rims, sparkled out from the dusky grime on his face; even the spit at the corners of his wide red mouth shone with life.

Now he sat, smoothly shaven, pristine clean, indoor-pale – and redundant. For the first time in my life I realised what that must mean to him. To have your skills rejected, to have nothing else to offer, to be pushed aside for the sake of progress; it must make you feel worthless. Like I felt now.

"You'll soon be home then," he whispered; the room was full of other patients and their visitors.

"Well, I might as well be, for all they're doing for me here." I spoke quite loudly.

"Shhh, our Lyn," he said, just like Kev had done, and he looked round nervously. "Think on. Remember how poorly you were afore." And he wagged a stubby finger.

"But I've recovered from that days ago. All I'm doing now is sitting in here being 'observed'. I feel like an animal in a laboratory."

"I can't quite see you as a guinea-pig; they're too round and cuddly. You're a bit of a whistler, though," he smiled.

He smiled?

He did.

I just had to smile back. "So how are you then, after all this upset? It's a pity Mam was busy and you had to see to everything – as usual." Oh, why wouldn't it come out right? I only meant to sympathise with him, to apologise for all the trouble I'd caused this week – this year – all my life.

"Aye, well, maybe it was just as well," he said softly.

I waited. There was obviously more to come, but he just sat and swirled his tea round the cup, staring into it.

"Tell your fortune then," I said.

"Eh?"

"You seem to be reading something down in that cup. I thought you were doing an Auntie Ede." Dad's sister had been a dab-hand with the tea-leaves.

"Aye, I could do with a peek into the future right now." He put the cup down and sat back, sighing. He placed a hand on each knee, gripping as if holding his legs down. Perhaps he had to hold them down to stop him running away.

"You can go, you know, whenever you like. After all, I'm not ill." I hoped he wouldn't, though.

"Nay, lass, I've come to see you and I'll stay for a bit."

I was beginning to see the point of set visiting hours; when the bell rang the poor visitors could get out. I remembered the battles we used to have to get to see our grandad.

Visiting hours were strictly limited to afternoons, and visitors to two. Grandad had at least twenty family and not one of them could get out to hospital in the afternoons. Mother, of course, took up the case, and it was bandied around the council chamber, the local papers – even local news on the telly, until the poor hospital committee crumbled. By that time, of course, Grandad was dead and my mother was on the Health Committee of the City Council.

Well, her fight for the Freedom of the Individual was costing my dad his freedom right now. He could be at home, brewing up, or slumped in front of the telly with Supergran.

"Can we go for a walk?" He suddenly stood up.

"What?" I was quite shocked.

"A walk – round the grounds like – or just to the cafeteria, if you don't want to go outside."

"We've just had tea," I reminded him. "And I've no coat." I knew that, because it had been one of the first things I'd looked for when I got up. In my locker was some underwear, a tracksuit and a pair of trainers. Not much chance of escape in that clobber.

"Ah, yes, I forgot. Well, we'll have to have an explore."

He hadn't said that word for years. When we were kids, Kevin and me, Dad would wrap us up in our anoraks and scarves, catch the bus right out to the moors, and start walking. "We'll go for a little explore, all on our own." And as we staggered along he'd show us the different land-forms, and tell us how they were made. While other kids were watching Saturday morning telly, we were plodding on in muddy wellies, looking at the evidence of the Last Ice-Age.

"The only fossils you'll find here are the living ones," I told him as we set off.

Again he smiled – even laughed a bit. I was so amazed that, for the first time, I even forgot all about my 'condition'.

We came to an open area, with pot-plants and leather sofas and low tables. It was quite deserted so Dad led me to a sofa away from the main corridor. As I sat down I noticed the sign over the reception desk. 'Family Planning Clinic', it said. 'Vasectomy Counsellor Thursdays 2 pm.' I wondered what Sister Willis would say if she saw us. I pointed to the sign; we both burst out laughing, only quietly so's not to attract attention. But laughing quietly only makes you laugh longer; we went on snuffling and giggling for quite some time, sharing Dad's brilliant white hanky to mop up with.

"Eeh, our Lyn, that's done me a power of good," he sighed.

"Well, something has, that's certain, Dad," I said, and waited.

"What happened, you see, when you were taken poorly, there was only me at home," he began.

"There always is."

"Aye, well, that's how I've been wanting it this past twelve-month. There's no wonder your mam's been buried in her work, there's been little enough for her to come home to a-lately."

"And she's had little enough time to come home a-lately." I said crisply. I can never resist the temptation of a witty remark, especially if it puts Mam down.

Dad didn't appreciate my humour. "Are you going to shut up and listen, or shall I tek meself off?" he demanded. He won't stand for cheek about Mam.

"Sorry, Dad. Go on then."

"Well, I was that shocked that I straightaway rang for a taxi, and by the time it arrived, I just had to get into it." He paused, seeming more amazed at his feat than I was.

"I'm ever so glad you did, Dad. It was grand to see you – even though I was half conscious."

He looked up then, and smiled at me – just the same smile

he used to have when we were collecting fossils and I got the right name for once. "Aye, well, you see . . . after that, I seemed somehow to be able to manage." I knew what he meant; he'd been shut up in the house for over a year. "And then, after they took you away, there wasn't anything we could do, so we went and had a cup of tea."

"We?"

"Aye, that Mr Baxter was here, if you remember."

Oh yes, I remembered very clearly Soupy's white, strained face peering over the trolley at me, and the way he dabbed my sweating face, and held my hand. Why had he not come to see me since? Perhaps he was embarrassed to meet me after that touching scene; it certainly made me blush. Luckily Dad was too busy to notice.

"Well, we got talking, like, and the upshot of it is, I'm going for a re-training course at the Adult Education Centre over in the Peak." Dad sat back, positively beaming. He seemed to think he'd finished the story.

I waited; this time I wanted to say the right thing. "Oh . . . er . . . good. What for?"

"For Geology, Botany, Ecology – all that sort of thing."

"I'm glad you've found something to fill up your time," I said cautiously. I felt relieved that he was actually getting out of the house, but I couldn't see how identifying flowers up the Peak was going to help an unemployed foundryman get another job.

"If I do well, it'll be more than passing the time. I s'll train to be a Ranger." He sat back in his chair and lifted his head higher than it had been since he lost his job.

As I watched him, I could feel the slight sickness, the absolute tiredness coming over me. Oh hell! Just when I wanted to show him . . . to tell him . . . I slumped forward.

"Come on, our Lyn, it's time you were back in bed – or something."

He almost lifted me up and together we staggered along the corridor.

Sister Willis was triumphant. "I told you to take tea in the Day Room," she chivvied Dad. "It's past Lyn's injection time and we couldn't find her anywhere."

Before they drew the curtains round my bed, I winked over at Dad. "Thanks for taking me on an explore," I said. "And good luck with the application. You look tons better already."

"I suppose it's the shock that's brought me to my senses," he said, patting my foot. "That and the case, of course. Poor Mr Baxter's in a hell of a state."

The curtain swooshed and he disappeared. What did he mean, 'the case'? And why was Soupy in a hell of a state? And why had he never been to see me?

As I assembled all my apparatus and found a nice, unlumpy bit of thigh to inject, I wondered what the hell was going on out there, in the real world. The sooner I joined it, the better.

Chapter 5

"Well, I think we've got a balance," announced Dr Ransome, a few days later. We were in her little office, going through the usual patter, and, as usual, I was only half listening; I'd heard it all many times, every day for the past week: grams and portions, energy and balance. I nodded vacantly and wondered whether I dared break out of the place.

"So you understand that, Lyn?"

"What?" I came to, sharpish.

"If you've got all your prescriptions you might as well go home today."

I didn't believe it. I think I didn't want to. It was one thing lounging around the hospital, moaning about being bored, feeling better, but knowing all the time there was the whole back-up of modern science behind you; quite another to be sent packing with a few gadgets and chemicals and your own self to be responsible for.

"You mean – home for good?" I asked.

"Well, I hope not; you'll have to strike out on your own some day," she smiled.

"But what about the – er – diabetes?" It was the first time I'd used the word.

"You know all about it, now. You can cope."

"But if anything goes wrong?"

"What can go wrong?"

"I don't know. You tell me."

"Things will only go wrong if you let them. Provided you follow the regime, you'll stay balanced. In any case I shall be seeing you as an outpatient every few weeks."

"Few weeks?" My voice rose and I was almost tearful.

"Well, starting next week," she conceded. "You're quite well now, you know."

"I'm not cured."

"There is no cure, Lyn, as you know. But there is a way of containing the problem. You should be glad of that."

"Oh yes, I'm thrilled." I sneered.

She ran her thin hand through her silky grey hair and stopped smiling. "You know what I mean," she said. "You have every chance of living a normal life; nothing need change, unless you were aiming to be a deep-sea diver, heavy goods driver or something?"

"Well, I had set my heart on working the oil-rigs," I said.

She ignored the childish sarcasm. "You can work anywhere, do anything, so long as you are well organised with the insulin and diet. Do you play sport?" she asked suddenly.

"No, I don't." I hate all that team stuff.

"You will need to find some form of exercise. It's a very important part of the treatment. Swimming, dancing, walking, jogging – anything which burns up sugar and keeps you fit. Think about it."

I thought about it and about the kind of folk who joined sports groups on our Wednesday options, all jolly and hearty together. I went to the library and had a good read or a scribble. When Soupy Baxter found me there he smiled and nodded in a friendly sort of way, then left me to it. We both knew he should have told me off and made me sign up for an activity but he never even mentioned it to me in tutorials. He's good like that, is Soupy.

"I go biking, or walking, out to the moors. That'll do me," I told Dr Ransome.

She sighed.

"You mustn't isolate yourself, Lyn. Diabetes is not contagious."

"So why did I get it?"

"We don't know; you may have a family tendency – your grandmother had it."

"So why me, and not our Kev? He's always been fat."

"Fat is only a side-issue. You mustn't let yourself get fat because it's unhealthy. It has nothing to do with your diabetes, unless you're already overweight. That's why exercise is important."

"Yeh, well, I get plenty of that walking to college and all."

"You should get out and meet people; make friends as you exercise – both will keep you well-balanced." I wasn't even looking at her; I didn't want to hear the brisk bits of advice. She sighed. "All right, Lyn. I'll see you at the clinic on Wednesday." She stood up and took my file off the desk. I could just see the word 'Bugge' creeping out from under her arm. "Do you need transport?"

I did not.

I went back to the ward; everybody was out – to the gym, or occupational therapy or treatments. I packed my sports bag; there were only my night things and all the college work my dear mother had sent. I could manage to get across town in my cagoule and track suit and trainers – we had to have trainers for the agonising gym sessions. There was a folder on my locker, with BDA stamped on it. It was called a Youth Pack, which made me giggle. "Many a Youth I've sent packing in my time," I could hear my gran saying. I shoved it into the bag, swung the bag on to my shoulder, and left.

At first I felt as if I'd just escaped from gaol; I expected a hand on my shoulder any moment. But – nothing, nobody even looked my way. It wasn't until I got to the entrance that I realised it was cold and wet and foggy. I stood looking out at the sodden hillside and remembered my last encounter with the elements. Well, they said I wasn't ill, now was my chance to prove them right – or wrong?

I joined the bus queue, which was so long that I was well beyond the sheltered bit. The drizzle drizzed, the cold gradually penetrated my track-suit, and when the bus arrived it wasn't a bus at all: it was a mini-coach. That's the trouble with free enterprise; it's all right for some. And it was; the first twelve people got on, didn't they? And you could argue that even I gained by that move: I just about shuffled under the bus-shelter. If I ducked my head every three seconds I even managed to avoid the heavy drips which slurped down from the roof.

What more could anybody ask for? I whistled a tune called 'The Best Things in Life are Free'. Dad and Kev and I used to sing that, plodding up the dale from a fossil hunt. I licked the rain off my lips, smelt the dankness in the fog, and was ten years old again.

"Lyn.... Lyn...." The voice wasn't from the past, it was coming from the car-park, opposite. I peered past my glasses, at the tall figure gesticulating in an inviting way. I slopped over, soaking my track-shoes in the ruts and puddles.

"Anna! what are you doing here?"

"I work here, remember? So what are you up to, then?"

"I'm going home, if ever the bus comes."

"Home? Like that?" She indicated my incredibly elegant outfit.

"It's all I've got."

"And you're wet through!" Suddenly she turned to the smart little Mini alongside. "Come on," she said, opening the driver's door.

"What are you doing? Whose is this car?" I asked.

"Get in, out of the rain, for heaven's sake, Lyn."

I hesitated. I had known a few joy-riders in my school, but they were always boys, and they usually operated at night. I looked round, expecting to be copped. Anna coolly flicked the passenger door open. "Get in!" she repeated.

"Me Mam allus tells me not to get into stranger's cars," I said, to cover my bewilderment.

"It's my mother's car; she lends it to me on hospital days." Anna started the engine. "I'll take you home."

"No!" I almost shouted. "You've got to get to work." Getting to work, in our family, was top priority; nothing, short of your own death, should interfere with that.

"Twenty minutes won't matter to the sluices and the corridors." She swung out of the car-park, past the even longer bus-queue. I saw the blank, waiting faces as we swished along. I felt guilty; I ought to have asked for a lift for two other people. But I couldn't, not in somebody else's car. I still felt guilty though; Mam would've insisted.

"So, you're out into the big world again, Lyn. How's it feel?"

Feel? I felt awkward, embarrassed, guilty... "All right," I answered. Then I had an inspiration. "Just drop me in the city; I can get the Flyer home, then you won't be late." The Flyers were free coaches that ran about the city.

"No, really, it's all right, Lyn. I can drop you at home and be back under half an hour." She changed the subject and closed the argument. "You coming in soon? To college?"

"Yeah, well, I expect so." I realised I'd not thought about it; not worked out about midday blood tests, injections and all.

"Because we need that extra material," she went on, zipping neatly round a lumbering van.

"What?"

"For the revue – the hospital sketches – you said you had some ideas."

"A few," I admitted. I had spent the past three days, sitting unobtrusively around various day rooms and wards, jotting down bits of conversation. They had sounded hilarious when I overheard them, but they looked so flat and boring when I read them later. I wasn't keen to show them to anybody.

"Well, if you could manage a production meeting, Friday afternoon? Do you good to pop in."

"That's your prescription, is it, Doctor Hitchens?"

"It is indeed, Madam Bugge," she replied in her best Mittel-European accent. "Vee 'ave ways of making you wurrk!"

And we laughed. It was odd how much laughing I seemed to do when Anna was around.

I relaxed and admired her driving, which, of course, was good.

"Well, I've got to come in to bring an essay for Ms Roberts and there's my project for Soupy."

There was a silence. Then, "Soupy's not in, didn't you know?"

"Don't tell me he's poorly too."

"No, not poorly." She copied the Yorkshire word absent-mindedly. "Oh, Lyn, they should have told you."

"Told me what?"

"Well, I thought perhaps your parents would have discussed it, or there might have been a letter... Do we turn right here?"

"Yes – and left at the next junction." I was remembering Dad's words, about 'the case' and poor Mr Baxter. I'd been so busy getting balanced since then, it seemed years ago since last Sunday. "Past the third lamp-post – on the right." Anna pulled the car in neatly. "So, what's all this about then?" I asked.

For the first time since I'd known her, Anna looked flustered.

"I thought you might have guessed, or somebody might have told you – I – er – oh hell!"

"Thank you for that crisp, concise summary of the situation, Dr Hitchens. We now return you to the studio," I said lightly, covering my alarm.

She laughed – rather nervously. "When we got back to college, after the field study week, Roger Baxter wasn't there."

"Who?"

"Roger – er – Soupy, as you Arts lot call him."

"Roger, indeed. I thought we 'arts lot' were the liberated ones."

"Roger – er – Mr Baxter, was one of my father's students; after... later he had a bed-sit at our house," she explained defensively.

"So... ?" I prompted. She seemed to be looking far ahead, up the road – or down the past?

"What? Oh, yes, well." Anna took a deep breath as though doing an exercise. "He wasn't there for classes so they sent a supply, who was worse than useless. I checked up on Roger but he wasn't at home. After a couple of wasted afternoons – you know – Tuesdays and Thursdays?"

I nodded. They were our Geog afternoons.

"I started making a few enquiries, and it was obvious that something was going on. I had to push through three layers of hierarchy before I discovered what it was."

Three layers of what? I didn't even know who was hierarchy at the college. But Anna Hitchens did.

"Mrs Harrison, Head of Humanities, Mr Cleaver, Dean of Faculty, Miss Patten, Principal," she chanted. "They all muttered about health and safety, but eventually Harri told me about the inquiry."

"What inquiry?" I enquired.

"The inquiry into your disappearance that night."

"I didn't disappear. I was on my way back."

"You were on your way to Featherbed Moss – and probable death."

I sat very still and thought about Dr Ransome. "What can go wrong?" she'd asked. Well, now I knew. "Probable . . .?" I whispered.

"Featherbed Moss is the toughest, most dangerous landscape on the Tops. It's just tussocks and peat bogs, you'd never have been able to walk there, in your condition, and the wind was bad that night – you'd have died from exposure, not the diabetes."

"You really mean that?" I made her look straight at me.

"Of course I do. Goodness, did they not tell you about the fatty reserves you have in your liver?"

"I don't know; they told me so much I haven't quite sorted it all out yet."

"You should join the BDA; they have lots of information."

"What's that?" I knew I'd seen those initials somewhere recently.

"British Diabetic Association. They're very helpful. But about Roger Baxter . . ."

I pulled myself together. I tried to look serious, though I felt more like grinning till my face split. I hadn't realised how frightened I was, until Anna talked so openly about dying – or rather, not dying.

She went on, "Apparently there's to be an inquiry into the incident and until it's over, Roger is suspended."

Elation ebbed away; I was suddenly cold and wet and exhausted. Anna waited for my reply; she was expecting an outburst, but I just didn't have it in me.

"I'm sorry, I didn't realise . . . I am sorry," I said feebly.

"Sorry? Lyn, it's not your fault; you were too ill to realise what was happening. And it's not Roger's fault, either; he couldn't have known . . . Well, we're not just sorry, we're furious and we're organising a . . ."

She turned to look at me. "Hey – you'd better get into your house and get something to eat. This has all been a shock and it's messing up your metabolism. Shall I help you in?"

"No, I can manage." I dragged myself and my bag out of the car. "Thanks for the lift, Anna. No! Don't get out – I can at least get up our path. Cheerio!"

And I stumbled up to our front door. Home at last!

Chapter 6

I plodded up the path, trying to remember what had happened to my key. Kev and I had our own keys in Junior School; in a family like ours you had to. I'd kept the same key for seven years, never lost it once, until now. I realised I hadn't seen it all the time I was in hospital and I'd never thought to ask about it. Oh hell! Now I'd have to ruin my casual, laid-back appearance at home, and knock on the door for Dad.

But I didn't. Before I'd even got up the path, the door was open and I rushed in.

"Steady on, our Lyn," said Gran. She pushed me into the house and slammed the door, as if to keep the world out. "I'll mash."

I flopped into Dad's chair and wondered vaguely where he was. I also wondered how I was going to get away from Gran to do my next blood-test. I shied away from the thought of the injection.

"Here y'are," said Gran. She brought in the teapot and set it on the hearth, in spite of the fact that we had a gas-fire now. "I'll just get cups and saucers." She brought the pots from the back kitchen, then went back again for the milk and sugar, and again for the biscuit tin. I watched her progress with amusement; I knew she didn't want me to help her.

"There's a marvellous invention, it'd save you all them trips," I said.

"Oh aye?"

"It's called a tray," I grinned.

"Still as cheeky as ever," she observed, swilling the tea round before she poured it.

You might have heard about the Japanese Tea Ceremony but I'll bet you've never heard of the Great Yorkshire Tea Palaver. Nobody in my family can simply put a tea-bag in a cup and pour boiling water on it. First comes the warming of the pot, then the mashing of the tea, then the repeated swishing of the fluid in the teapot, to ensure maximum strength. Next, the bottom of the cups are drowned in sterilised milk and half filled with thick brown fluid from the pot. At this point the pot must be 'knocked back' to jerk the fluid to life before topping up. Finally, heaped spoonsful of white sugar are plonked in, and the whole noxious liquid stirred vigorously. This last must be performed by the female who is mashing; in Yorkshire, no real man stirs his own tea.

I don't like tea.

"'Ere y'are then." After the ceremonial, Gran passed a cup and saucer over to me.

I took it and sipped. Then I remembered. "Gran, have you sugared?" I hoped she'd understand.

She did. "Oh, dammit, I have that. Ne'er mind, I'll do another."

"Just pour me a glass of milk – that'll do," I said.

Eventually we were settled, either side of the fire-place,

with the biscuit tin on the floor between us. After two glasses of milk and some digestives, I was feeling quite well again, until I remembered I'd have to count that snack in with my dinner portion. Even the tiniest of nibbles were added into my daily allowance.

"Where's me dad?" I asked her.

"Off retraining or whatever it's called."

"What time does he get back?"

"Teatime." Gran's clock only registered four times: breakfast, dinner, tea and bed.

"Oh good," I said, feeling happy that he'd find me home.

"Sat'day," she added.

"What?"

"He comes home every Sat'day teatime."

I was shocked. I'd listened to his plans up at the hospital, but I didn't think they'd affect the family; no, let's be honest, I didn't think he'd see them through. "I didn't know he was starting so soon," I complained.

"Best go while he could. He's lost enough time as it is." Gran didn't believe in Depression.

I grinned at her and felt a bit less sorry for myself. Gran has that effect on me. That's another little difference of opinion between Kev and me: Gran irritates him. She doesn't even have to say anything to him; just by being at our house, cleaning and scrubbing (yes, she still does that!) and dusting, she grates on his nerves. He's so possessive about our house, you'd think he owned it.

"And where's our Kev?" I asked her.

"I don't rightly know; he went off out just after I got here. I'nt it his day?" She meant for signing on.

We both knew that even if it wasn't his day, he wouldn't stay in with her in charge.

We cleared up – using the tray – and I helped her to wash

the pots. It was very soothing to be doing jobs with my grandma, like I did when I was little.

When I'd finished I sat at the kitchen table and watched Gran fettling round the sink. Nobody can leave a kitchen sink like our Gran. First she washed it all round with green soap, then she rinsed it, then she mopped up the water; finally she washed out the tea-towel I'd just used, dried out the sink with it, and hung it on the rail by the boiler. The steel sink and draining-board shone like the family silver we'd never had. Whenever I came in the back way, I could tell if Gran had been round: a clear, shining draining board was her sign.

"Life's too short to polish sinks," our Mam said. And to iron sheets, darn socks, cook Sunday dinner... collect your daughter from hospital.

As if she read my thoughts Gran said, "Your mam won't be back till late. You'd best sort yourself out while I get a bit of dinner ready." Trust Gran to understand.

Up in my room I unpacked the bag. I put all the gadgets in a line on my desk. It was well past midday and I hadn't even done a test. I took a packet of strips and went off to the lavatory. If I'd thought about it at all, I'd assumed you had to pee into a jar to do a urine test. But, thankfully, you don't. You just hold the little strip of paper into the stream of pee; it's dead easy, so long as you hold on to the strip. When I'd done, I checked it against the shade chart: it was already higher than my last test at the hospital. I went back to my room to perform the blood test. I took a lancet and pressed it on my thumb. I didn't even feel the prick, but my hands were shaking as I pressed the globule on to the tip of the strip. I counted thirty seconds, wiped off the blood, and peered at the colour of the indicator. Pale blue for low sugar, deepest red for high. Guess which one was me? And I hadn't even seen Mam yet.

I'd been so confident, in hospital, but here at home I felt cack-handed. I took out the little bottle of insulin, punctured the lid with the sterile needle and drew the fluid down into the syringe. I quite liked this bit, like playing doctors-and-nurses. I did not like the next bit so I acted quickly. I pulled my track suit bottoms down, pinched a bit of thigh and jabbed in the needle, ejecting the fluid at the same time. All over in seconds.

I let out a juddering breath, and rested my head against the mirror. I couldn't imagine being expert enough to do that in front of anyone.

The door flew open and our Kev said, "So how did you get home, then?"

Not "How are you?" or "Welcome home."

"Shhhhit!" I screamed, pulling up my trousers. "Gerrout, you!" I was nearly crying with – with what? Temper, fury, but with something else too: shame.

He backed out, but just before he shut the door, he put his head round. "I'm just going to ring our Mam. I'll tell her you're back."

I turned to the wall and cried.

When we were little, Kev and I were very close. Dad used to laugh at us, playing in the park, me never off my bike and Kev collecting little stones, leaves, twigs, and arranging them in neat patterns on a bench. While I was running around the allotments with my gang, Kev was running off to the corner shop for something nice for tea.

"A pair of wrong 'uns, you two," Grandad would say. "You're t'wrong way round; Ladlass Lyn, and Lasslad Kev." And we used to giggle together about our secret names. We never told anybody, though; South Yorkshire's a good place for 'manny' girls but it's hell for gentle boys.

'Yer gret woman!' is a term of abuse for anybody who can't heave a railway sleeper or shift ten pints at dinner time.

My stomach rumbled at the thought of dinner. I went downstairs, where the smell of cabbage was strong. Gran's a great housewife, but she can't cook. Kev looked up from the settee, and raised an eyebrow elegantly; he's a very good cook.

"I did offer, our Sis, but you know what she's like," he whispered.

It was a peace-offering.

"What's she doing?" I asked, though I knew the answer.

"Steak-and-kidney out of a tin, boiled cabbage and lumpy potatoes," he grinned. "Welcome home."

I think he meant it.

It was nearly nine when Mam got in. I heard a car pull up, then the click of her heels up the path; Kev jumped up to let her in.

"Hello, love," she said to me. "Sorry I've been so long getting home, but it's all hell at the City Hall. Anyway, you've settled in, then?"

"Gran was here, she helped," I said pointedly.

"Ah well, she would," Mam agreed.

"Have you eaten anything, Mam?" asked Kev, all solicitous. "We've had tuna salad because of Gran's stodgy dinner." I wasn't the only one in our family who had to count the calories. Kev easily runs to fat.

"Make us some real coffee, Kev, that'll do me." And he shot off into the kitchen, happy as Larry.

She sat down and eased her high heels off, stretching her legs and twitching her toes. She'd got good legs, good figure, good brain – everything.

"Well then, Roslyn, you're all well again, I gather." She didn't ask, just 'gathered'.

"Well as can be expected, I think the phrase is."

She ignored the joke. (What joke? I wasn't joking.) "So you can get back to college tomorrow, can't you?"

"I am getting back, to take my work in. I'll start back on Monday."

"Well, that's up to you." She always said this before she tried to run somebody else's life. "But there's no point in a wasted day, is there? If you're going up to take the work in, you might as well stay on for your lectures."

I didn't answer. There's no point arguing with somebody who's always right. And anyway, I never discussed college matters with her; I certainly was not going to mention the production meeting, or Anna. That'd give her all sorts of ideas above my station.

Kev brought a thick jug of clear, black coffee and three mugs. They always drank theirs black, those two, but I liked frothy boiled milk in mine, and sugar.

"You'll have to use Mam's sweeteners," he said.

"Who the hell do you think you are?" I asked him. "You're worse than any bossy nurse."

"I picked up a leaflet about it in Boots. If you can't manage without sugar, we'll get some sweeteners for you."

"Balls!" I muttered from the kitchen, where I deliberately scooped up two huge sugars and slopped full-cream milk into my mug. I sat at the kitchen table stirring noisily so that the coffee looked like a storm at sea. There was no sound from the room next door.

When they turned the television on, for the news, I went in, meaning to go up to my room, but, as usual, unable to pass the box without peering over the settee.

I got a shock. On the screen was the drive up to college, with a crowd of students milling about. I noticed Gary Baldwin and Anna laughing together.

"Hey, Sis, it's your place," Kev said.

"Shhh!" Mam hissed. I went to join them on the settee. On the screen Anna moved forwards and began to speak.

"That's your friend from the hospital," said Kev.

"Shhhh." Mam and me both hit him.

"The S.U. feels that there has been no consultation in this matter. We are not prepared to work with a supply lecturer. If necessary we will work privately with Mr Baxter, who is, after all, supervising our examination work."

"But do you accept there was negligence on the field study trip?" the reporter asked her.

I waited for Anna to wither him.

"That is a matter for the authorities to investigate."

I gasped. "Investigate – what does she mean?"

"Shhhh!" Kev slapped my knee.

"So you are protesting about Mr Baxter's suspension, not his innocence?"

"Our point is that we need Mr Baxter's expertise to follow up a crucial field study. And we need that now, not in six months time."

Then the camera cut away to the rest of the crowd and Gary stuck a finger right into the lens. End of story.

"Well, there's fame for you," said Kev, over the weather forecast.

I remembered Dad's words: "Poor Mr Baxter's got enough on with that inquiry." And Anna's uneasiness that morning in the car. "Somebody should have told you."

Somebody should, they bloody well should.

I looked along at Mam. "Why didn't you tell me about all this?" I asked quietly.

"It's only just broke into the news," she said.

"But it's all been happening out of the news while I've been in hospital."

"It's not been generally known."

"What, not even at City Hall?" I didn't believe she'd be kept out of this.

She got up and turned off the television, ignoring, for once, Kev's protest. "I'm not on the Education Committee."

"But you must have known this was going on. Dad knew."

"Oh . . . Dad . . ." She bunched up her hair with her hand, and yawned.

Perhaps she really was tired; as it turned out later, she had plenty to be tired about. But to me that dismissive yawn was infuriating.

"Don't you talk like that about my dad!" I shouted. I hadn't meant to shout, but now that the telly was off, my voice came out all loud.

"I wasn't talking about him, you were," she reminded me. She stood over me, looking down into my face. "Look, Lyn, you were poorly, you needed to get to grips with this diabetes, I didn't want anything to get in the way of that. Now you're balanced, you need to stay balanced. You've got to keep on an even keel, at least until the exams are over."

That summed her up; nothing must get in the way of her/my success. Somtimes I think she doesn't see me at all, only her own wasted youth on the shop-floor. She worked hard to fight her way out, but she'll never get any further in her job, without a degree. I've got to be her next success.

"But Soupy – Mr Baxter. He's in trouble because of me."

"Not because of you, Lyn, because of his own carelessness. God, he only had twelve of you to look after. Couldn't he even count?" She sounded so bitter I looked up amazed. She turned away and dropped her hair around her face. "I'm whacked," she said. "I'm going to have a bath." She pressed the telly button on again, smiled at Kev and padded upstairs minus her shoes.

Kev picked one up and stroked it. "She was sick with worry the night you went missing. I mean, spewing."

"So was I."

"She feels guilty, you know," he said, putting both shoes meticulously together on the floor. They looked fragile by the side of his baggy trainers.

"Guilty? What about?" I was really puzzled. Mam never had any time for feelings; so long as she was working – onwards and upwards – she seemed so confident, so sure of everything.

"Well, I suppose she passed this diabetes on to you from her mother."

"Aw heck – that's possible, but I could just as easily be the first one in the family to have it; there were some folk at the hospital who had no known connection."

"But you have."

"Our Mam."

He nodded, thoughtfully. We sat in silence, listening to the pipes bumping as Mam filled her bath. There'd be no more hot water tonight.

"I thought she didn't care," I said finally.

"Ay well, she allus does that when she's worried; plays it cool, like, especially where you're concerned. See, she wants such a lot for you, does Mam."

"From me, you mean."

"No I don't. She wants all the things for you that she's missed out on: education, university, a real career . . ."

"What about a real mam? Seems to me we've both missed out on that."

"Seems to me you've missed out on the last ten years of women's rights. What the hell do you mean by a 'real mam'? Somebody in a pinny who bakes bread and washes with Persil? So what does that make me?"

I pushed my glasses up my nose and looked at him. Not a

pretty sight. Kev's golden curls stood round his plump pink face, echoed by the ginger stubble round his cheeks. He looked like a rather mature cherub. I grabbed a few curls and tugged on them. "That'll do, our lad," I said.

"Nobbut just, our lass," he answered, heavily.

Then we both took a fit of the giggles and collapsed on the settee.

He's the best bloke I know, is our Kev. Well, next to our Dad.

Chapter 7

I was cured! No more injections, no more diets and grams and tests. I often had those dreams in the early days: a mistaken diagnosis and I was back to normal.

As soon as I woke, I knew I was not. I lay in bed, half asleep, trying to drag up the energy to sit up and do a blood test. I failed, and slept some more. When I surfaced again, my room was full of brilliant sunshine and the noise of banging.

"Wake up, our Lyn, else I'm coming in!" Kev was sounding very agitated about something.

"I am awake – shurrup and gerroff," I replied in my usual charming manner.

"Well, get up, then. You should have had a blood test and an injection two hours ago."

"What time is it?" I was suddenly interested.

"Ten thirty."

"Oohhh – hell and damnation." I staggered out of bed, feeling worse than I did earlier. "And stop that banging!"

"Can I come in? I've got some tea." He didn't wait for an

answer; he came in bearing the tray ahead of him, balanced on one hand, like a professional waiter. He placed the tray beside me on the bed and drew back the curtains. "Bonjour, madame," he exclaimed, wrong as usual.

The sun flooded the room now, outlining Kev's fuzzy head in a halo, making him appear so clean, so energetic, so healthy that I groaned. I felt dull, lethargic and sick.

"Come on, Lyn, drink that tea and eat two digestives. That'll help."

"How do you know, Doctor Clever-Clogs?" I dunked a biscuit and sucked the squishy half.

"I've been reading all about it in your stuff."

"What stuff?" I gulped the hot tea without tasting it.

"That folder – from the BDA; you left it downstairs last night so I read it. More tea?" He played mother and refilled my mug.

"So you're the diabetes expert, are you?" I asked.

"No, but I've learnt a lot. You should read that folder. It's very useful."

"I've heard it all, at the hospital."

"Yes, but you haven't remembered everything. This, for instance." He waved an arm towards the tea-tray.

"How to make tea, in three easy lessons? Of course I have."

"Very funny; you know what I mean."

Actually I didn't. "Well what?"

"You mustn't sleep in and miss an injection – point one. You should have a drink and a snack by your bedside, to take as soon as you wake up – point two. You might need a long-lasting insulin for overnight, if you feel badly in the morning – point three."

I sighed. "I felt that much better last night, Kev, I even thought I might be cured. Now it's all here again."

"It won't be cured, you know that, nump. But it'll go

away, if you just follow the regime. Now, I'll get out of your way while you get up." He collected the tray, brushed the crumbs off the bed, and left, trailing clouds of sunshine. Whatever became of grumpy old Kev?

I wasn't late to college because I wasn't officially there at all. But as soon as I did arrive, I walked straight into trouble. I went across to the Arts Building but before I could get in, a woman blocked my way. She looked as if she'd escaped from combat, all khaki dungarees, Doc Marten's and a tape-recorder slung across her chest. She pounced, like a little predatory animal – a weasel maybe, and waved a microphone up to my face.

"Miss Bugge? Roslyn?" Mesmerised, I gave a frozen sort of nod. So she pushed on swiftly. "We're interested in your response to the suspension of Mr Baxter." I just stood there. "You are aware that as a result of your disappearance on the field course, Mr Baxter has been suspended?" I looked past her to the entrance, sizing up the chances of shoving her out of the way. She was a pretty hefty lady, though.

"Our listeners are keen to hear your side of things. Is it true that you almost died of hypothermia?" She prattled on, still firmly between me and the entrance I needed. Who the hell was she?

A few other people arrived and stood around watching and cutting off my exit behind. Suddenly I felt hemmed in, began to sweat, even in the mean wind that always blew round the Arts Block. I looked left, down the steps to the main drive. A Radio Sheaf van was parked there; hers, no doubt. She was still blabbing on about enquiries and rights, thrusting her microphone into my face, and fiddling with her tape-recorder.

I saw my chance and dodged past her to the big revolving doors. I intended to dash through the doors, then swing them hard and disappear down the corridor. It was a dodge that often worked when I wanted to escape from chatty students or pressing lecturers.

But under pressure my timing was bad. Or else she was nimbler on her feet than I thought. Anyway, we both ended up in the same section of the huge swing door, which immediately stopped swinging and stuck.

"Brilliant," grinned the reporter. "Now will you speak?" And she waved her microphone up to my face. Only it didn't quite reach; the cable was jammed in the edge of the door.

I looked around the little glass booth. I groaned and leaned heavily on the partition; it never budged.

As requested, I spoke. "How will we get out?" I asked.

She shrugged. "I expect my driver will send for a caretaker or somebody." Then she giggled. "Quel joke, eh? Mind you, I can think of several people I'd rather be trapped with than you. No offence, mind."

"Much taken, I'm sure. I suppose you realise that if you'd let me pass, neither of us would be stuck here?"

"You could argue that if you'd answered my simple questions. . . ."

"Oh, come on!" I was getting hotter and sweatier every second. "You're asking me to make a statement about an official inquiry when I'm not even invited to appear?" Shiiit! I could have bitten my tongue off.

"You mean you have not been approached by the governors?"

"I haven't been at college this week," I backtracked.

"Didn't anyone official from the college visit you, whilst you were in hospital?"

"What? Oh . . . yes. Of course they did." Well, Anna was President of the SU.

"Who was that?"

"I'm not telling you everything that goes on in college," I

said. The glass partitions were steamed up now. I rubbed one to clear a patch and peered out. People were surrounding the entrance, but nobody seemed to be doing anything to release the door. I hammered on the glass, but only hurt my hands.

"Better relax; you look very pink," said the reporter. "Try some deep breathing."

I ignored her and leaned my head on the cold door. Ever since I was a kid, I've hated small spaces; I'd walk up hundreds of steps to avoid a lift, and cross my legs rather than go into Gran's outside lav. I never knew why I did this until now. My stomach ached with anxiety, I felt sick, and the sweat trickled down my back. Alone, I would have panicked, but with Miss Noseyparker in there with me, I was determined not to give way.

She tugged up her microphone again. "Go on," she encouraged. "Just tell our listeners your side of the story. You'll have to stoop down to the mike."

I couldn't believe this woman; we were stuck in that infernal machine and all she could do was produce her damned mike. I was breathing deeply by this time; not with relaxation, with fury. I wrenched the mike from her and held it high above my head out of her reach. "Mind the cable..." she yelled. But even as I pulled, a frayed length of wire sprang between us and we both jerked away.

The door gave a lurch, one swing, and flung us both on the entrance-hall floor. I got up and ran, clutching my files to my chest as if they were top secret.

I expected to find Anna and her cast rehearsing in the studio. But thank God it was empty. I flopped down on a tip-up seat and tried to get my breath back. But no matter how deeply I breathed, I couldn't stop sweating and shaking. If college life was going to be as exciting as this, I'd have to opt out, that's all. Come to that, if real life was going to be . . .

"Well, there you are!" Anna came in, followed by three girls. "My God, Lyn, is all your whole life packed with incident or does it only happen when I'm around?"

But before I could get it together to speak, a couple of youths rushed in. One was Gary Baldwin. "Lyn!" he boomed. "You've got to report to admin straight away. There's all hell on up there."

Everybody looked at me. I wished they wouldn't. I wished they'd all go away and leave me alone. I wished I'd never come back.

"You all right, Lyn?" Anna asked. I wished she wouldn't.

I nodded, stood up and thrust the files at her.

Walking up the steps out of the studio was like walking through treacle. As soon as I got through the door I tried to rush to the lavatories; at least it felt like rushing. When I finally made it I locked myself in the nearest one and set out the paraphernalia on my knee.

Sugar high – of course. No need for a blood test, the urine said it all. Hypodermic into phial, needle into thigh, all done – except where to put the used needle? Not a good idea to leave it in the bin outside; might start a drugs panic amongst the staff. I looked at the sani-bin; I wasn't sure how they disposed of those things; what if the hypo needle punctured any plastic container? Oh damnation – all that talk at the hospital and nobody mentioned this problem. I sat there, on the lidded lav, looking at the offensive weapon. I could have cried.

Instead I started giggling. I mean, there was I, supposed to be answering a summons from on high, sitting on the lav with a disposable needle in my hand, trying to dispose of it. Of all the problems I had at that moment, only one concerned me. Where should I put the blasted needle?

Still laughing, I pulled a dozen sheets of paper off the roll, wrapped the hypo round and round until it was well padded, then, holding it in my palm, against my side, I cautiously unlocked the door and peered out. Nobody there. I shot across the tiles and dropped the thing into the wastebin. Humming nonchalantly, I washed my hands, rubbed my hair, adjusted my glasses and set off to admin – whoever that was. Now, I felt fine!

"Mr Cleaver will see you now."

The secretary who showed me in gave nothing away; she was soo coool . . . as I passed her at the door I sneezed, she smelt so expensive. "Miss Bugge has arrived, sir," she said, implying 'at last'.

"Ahh – right – yes – Miss Bugge. Come in."

I was in. He was a big man; as big as our Dad, but with a pasty, floppy face, like some Americans. He half stood as I walked in, grasping the arms of his chair and lifting his big buttocks off the seat.

"Sit down," he ordered, nodding at the chair across the desk from him.

I'd heard our Mam going on at length about office games, so I pulled the chair away from his area of authority, into the middle of the room. Then I sat down. First point to me.

"Now, Miss Bugge – may I call you Roslyn?"

"No."

"Oh? May I ask why not?" His eyes were steely light blue.

"They call me Lyn." I still held his gaze, though.

"Lyn, right." He looked away. Another point to me. There was a pause.

"Well, now, I expect you've been wondering what's going to happen?"

"About what?"

"About your – er – accident."

"No."

"Oh, we rather thought you might be worrying about coming back into college."

"No, I'm not," I lied.

"Then again, we were rather surprised to see you on the premises today. We had been informed that you would be back on Monday."

"I will."

"So why did you arrive today?" For the first time he frightened me. I was just playing the usual game: monosyllables, dumb insolence, until then, but now I felt he was wise to that.

"To bring in some work for Ms Roberts and Mr Baxter," I answered. I didn't want to tell him about my writing.

"But instead you got yourself interviewed by a local reporter."

"As well as . . ." I murmured. I hoped Anna would have the sense to pass my work-files in.

"What?"

"Not instead of bringing the work, as well as."

"Well, if we're being so accurate . . ." I'd obviously succeeded in rattling him. Was that a point to me? I was no longer sure.

Mr Cleaver spread his hands and bounced his fingers off each other. "So, you told the reporter that you had not been asked to make a statement about the accident to the governors?"

How the hell did he know that? Did he have the revolving door bugged? No, doubtless that scummy reporter had already been in for questioning. I nodded, staring him out. It didn't work this time.

"But that isn't true. You made a statement to the police, from the hospital." I nodded again. "That statement is the one I have put before the governors. It was quite adequate for our purposes." He smiled, showing surprisingly sharp little teeth.

I couldn't even remember what I'd said that night when they finally settled me into the hospital. "Can I see it?" I asked.

"Do you want to change it?"

"I don't know, until I read it."

"I'm not convinced that will be necessary; after all, you made the statement to the police, and signed it; they accepted it in good faith, so shall we."

"But I was exhausted and ill then . . ."

"Ah, so you do admit that?"

"What do you mean?" I knew he was playing games again, but I couldn't work out his rules.

"There seems to be an attempt to play down the seriousness of your situation. These student activists, campaigning for Mr Baxter's return, they seem to imply that it was a mere mishap."

I pondered this for a moment. I still didn't understand what he was at. "Well, accident, mishap, what's the difference?" I asked cautiously.

"A difference of degree, perhaps?" He sounded like one of those silky smooth prosecutors in a TV courtroom. Mr Cleaver – hadn't Anna mentioned him? – 'hierarchy', she'd said. What did that make him? Not the Principal; even I knew her name. I tried my best glare across the room at him, regretting now I was so far away.

"Did you see the local news on television last night?" he went on casually, as if asking about an episode of *Neighbours*.

"Yes."

"Yes. And thought, no doubt, that you might as well add your penn'orth to the argument?"

"No – I've told you. I came in to bring my essays and . . ."

There was a pause. Mr Cleaver sighed. "The point is,

Lyn, that your presence here is going to arouse all sorts of irrelevant emotions. I suggest you take another week's leave, until all the fuss dies down." He began to collect papers together, as if everything had been settled.

"But I don't need a week's leave. I'm not ill," I said.

"Really?" He looked down at his papers – my papers – again. "I gather you are to attend as an out-patient on a regular basis; healthy people don't do that."

I was sickened. I could have vomited all over his desk, his papers, him. Hadn't Dr Ransome assured me that I wasn't ill? That once I was balanced there was nothing I couldn't do? That diabetes is not an illness?

"It's not an illness," I stood up and shouted at him. "I'm as fit as you are – fitter by the pasty looks of you. And I can't afford to miss another week's lectures and I have no more work set and I have exams and . . . I . . ." Oh stupid, stupid, stupid. Even though these were tears of fury in my eyes, he had seen them, and chose to misinterpret them.

"You are obviously not quite fit yet. Another week at home will do you good. I shall see that work is provided, so that you don't fall behind."

Now he stood up and came out from behind his desk to tower over me. "If the governors feel they need further information from you they will send for you. But unless they do, I must ask you to stay off the college premises all next week."

He looked straight at me, his cold eyes puncturing my feeble anger, leaving me dry-mouthed and drippy-eyed. "Does that mean I'm suspended too?" I had the wit to ask.

"I am merely telling you to keep away from the stress of an unpleasant situation. I'm sure your doctors would agree that stress is bad for your – er – condition. And by the way,

Lyn, journalists are very stressful people – you should avoid them, too."

He walked past me and opened the door. "I think that covers everything. Goodbye, Lyn, and thank you for being so reasonable." He ushered me out. "Mrs Canning will ring for a taxi, to save you any more hassle." And he nodded towards the scented lady, who was already on the phone.

I've often wondered how brave I'd be in a really tough situation. You know, like in the film, when the Nazi murmurs "Vee have vays . . ." or the terrorist holds a knife to your throat. I used to be quite daring when I was a little girl. I was always small for my age but tough with it; they didn't call me Ladlass Bugger for nothing.

But then I sat down in that office, drank the coffee Ms Scenty gave me and waited for the taxi to arrive like the goody-good child I never had been.

"Taxi – for Norton Estate?" The driver poked his head round the door, and Mrs Canning nodded graciously towards me. Numb, I followed him down the corridor for a few seconds, until I realised we were going the wrong way.

"The entrance is over there," I called, pointing back.

"Aye, but my cab's round the service entrance, duck. I couldn't get anywhere near t'front."

So, I'd be smuggled out without a chance to see anybody. Real KGB stuff. And what was that man who'd just interviewed me? I was a fool not to demand to know his rank. The very thought of that made me giggle.

"All right, me duck?" asked my driver. "Been tekken poorly, have you?"

"No, I have not!" I snarled at him.

We walked past the kitchens, past the boiler-rooms, out to

the back courtyard to his cab. To my surprise, he opened the door for me as if I was somebody really important.

"Careful where you put your feet, me duck," he said.

When I got in, I realised what he meant. There was no room for my feet because the whole floor was taken up by Anna Hitchens.

Chapter 8

"What larks then, eh, Lyn?" said Anna, misquoting from my A-level set text. Now that we were clear of college, she was sitting next to me on the back seat of the taxi.

"What are you doing here? Where are we going?" I asked as the driver took us across the roundabout and to the ring-road instead of turning down towards the city.

"We'll take one question at a time, young lady. I think that would be fair." She puffed out her cheeks and bared her teeth in a good imitation of Cleaver.

"Yes - that's just like him," I laughed. "What is he, anyway?"

"You mean he didn't even tell you? Oh that's typical of college administration. He's Colin Cleaver, Dean of Faculty. He's chairing the hearing next week."

I went cold all over. I'd no idea what a Dean of Faculty did, but it sounded far too important to be glared and shouted at by a mere student. "I thought he was just some sort of admin bloke," I muttered.

"That just about sums him up," agreed Anna. "So what did you say to him?"

When I told her she leaned back and shook with laughing. "Oooh, Lyn, you're an *enfant sauvage* all right!" she gulped.

The taxi pulled into a street of old stone houses. It was only then that I thought about paying. I'd only got my bus-fare and a pound over for dinner. But Anna airily got out, held the door for me, and waved the taxi on.

"Clever old Cleaver ordered the taxi," she explained. "He'll pay for it."

I followed her up the short path to the porch. I knew we must be somewhere in the university area; all the houses around there were stone-built, detached, and big. Just the sort of place for Anna's family.

At the end of a long passage was a big kitchen. It wasn't a neat, fully-fitted kitchen like ours. It had old cupboards right down to the floor on one side, a big cream Aga on another, and a long table with wooden chairs round it right in the middle. The floor was red-tiled, and not very clean, I noted, with Gran's eyes.

Anna picked up a heavy old kettle and lifted the shiny lid of one of the hotplates. "Coffee?" she asked, plonking the kettle down. "We'll have a bit of lunch too, I think. Sandwich do you?"

I sat down at the long table; it would seat eight, though there were only four chairs set round it. "Have you got a big family?" I asked.

"Sometimes, when everybody's home. Why do you ask?"

I nodded at the table.

"Oh, that's the council table," she laughed. "It was Mum's work-bench but it's always been the family meeting-place."

"What does your mother do?" I looked at the table-top

curiously. It was cut and hacked, stained and painted.

"Designs," said Anna briefly. She set a board on the table and started cutting a little brown loaf.

"You mean dresses?" I asked.

Anna gurgled her low, soft laugh. "Heavens no!" she answered. "Sets."

"Sets of what?"

"Sets, Lyn, as in the theatre – you know? How many – one or two?"

"One," I answered, wanting two. They were very little slices.

Anna looked at me. "How many grams?" she tested.

"Depends what you put in it," I prevaricated. Actually I had no idea.

"Cheese-and-Branston? OK? I'll just do a few and you can help yourself." She continued cutting, spreading and slicing the cheese, assembling the sandwiches with neat efficiency. I wanted to offer to help, but didn't know how. "Kettle's just about boiled," she said briskly. "Coffee's over there, mugs on the draining-board – you make it." And she left me. I could hear her pounding upstairs and calling. Perhaps her mother was designing somewhere in the house.

I collected two mugs; the least stained ones. Gran would have had a gala day bleaching this lot, I thought. The sink was piled high with pots and pans awaiting washing. It would never have been allowed at home.

I'd just made the coffee when Anna came back. "Make another," she commanded.

And Soupy Baxter walked in.

"Hello, young Lyn, are ye feeling better than last time we met?" He grinned, and for the first time I noticed how young he was. I mean at college – even on the Field Study Course – he had always been the one in charge so he'd seemed a lot older than us. Seeing him now, in Anna's kitchen, his boney face pink, his black hair damped down, perhaps from a recent bath, he looked about sixteen.

I wanted to say something casually witty, something about his predicament – our predicament – which would comfort and amuse him. "I'm all right," I said. Such wit! Such repartee! "Coffee?"

"Thanks, that'd be great. Shouldn't you be in college today?" He turned to Anna.

"You might well ask, Roger," said Anna, passing over the bread board of sandwiches to him. "Go on, Lyn, tell him," she commanded.

"Well, er, yes." Oh God, why was I always so incoherent? I gulped, breathed deeply, and began. "I did go in but there was a kerfuffle – reporter from Sheaf radio – and I tried not to say anything but I was sent to Sir and now I'm suspended."

Soupy blinked fast, like a startled schoolboy. "But they can't do that; you've done nothing wrong." He picked up another sandwich and chewed on it viciously.

"Exactly!" Anna pounced on his words. "Now they really have overstepped the mark. We were on dicey ground, demonstrating on your account; you have your own union after all. But now we have victimisation of a fellow-student – we've got them!" She brandished the remains of her bread like a miniature flag. "What's more important, we've got Cleaver."

I didn't say anything. I was upset about Cleaver's attitude, but I didn't want to be ammunition for anybody's campaign. Anna was like my mother; she would use anything, any person, as an excuse to form a committee and fight for the cause. Any cause.

"Lyn may not want a fight," observed Soupy, sipping his coffee and reading my mind.

"Oh, come on, Lyn, you wouldn't refuse to fight for

Soupy's reinstatement, would you," Anna stated rather than asked.

"Well, er, no. Of course not," I answered, unconvinced and unconvincing. "But I've only been told to stay at home another week; that's probably not worth fighting over."

"If it's against Cleaver, it's worth fighting over. It's the principle that counts."

Whenever I hear anybody say that, I know the argument is over. Our Mam says that every time she has a 'discussion' with Dad.

"How's your dad now, is he going off to the Peak?" asked Soupy, telepathically. He turned to me; dissolving my guts as he caught my eye.

"Oh, er, yes, mmmm, well." Shhii . . . I took a deep breath and started again. "Thanks to your suggestion, he's already made a start. He's not due home until tomorrow tea-time so I don't know . . ." Tears started to my eyes, I could have died with embarrassment; why the hell did that happen?

"You must miss him," Soupy said sympathetically. He hadn't missed the tears.

I shook my head, but I couldn't explain. It was just the thought of our Dad, sitting at home for all that time, too broken even to go out. I was only too glad to miss that.

"Order! Order!" Anna rapped on the table. "AOB and dads at the end of the agenda."

But I couldn't take any more. I got up and rushed to the door.

"Lyn! Where are you going?" Anna demanded.

"Upstairs, turn left – it's at the end of the passage," said Soupy.

I washed my hands and face in the bathroom and stood gazing into the mirror. What was the matter with me? Surely the sugar level couldn't have this emotional effect?

I'd been so cool, in public, before all this; nobody – but nobody – ever saw me cry. Oh, I was pretty sharp and often grotty tempered, but never wet, never weak. Now I seemed to be near to tears every hour. Well, I'd just have to watch out, toughen myself up, avoid emotional situations, as Mam said.

I went back to the kitchen and announced that I'd have to get home.

"Why?" asked Anna, disappointed in me (another one!). "Nobody's expecting you, are they?"

Unfortunately she was right. I sat down at the end of the table, a long way from Soupy, and listened to Anna.

"So, I'll run an article in our newspaper, and syndicate it to the locals. I'll insist on seeing Cleaver, first thing Monday, and meantime put out feelers for the General." She meant Ms Patten, the Principal. "It's my turn to get going now, I really ought to be back there." She looked from one to the other of us, wondering how to organise her dependants.

"Take my bike," Soupy urged her.

"Oh, could I? Thanks, Roger – wow – your precious Mountain Bike, there's an honour." She looked over to me. "Oh, what about Lyn?" she asked, as if I was an infant.

Soupy looked at me too. "She'll be all right with me. Even I couldn't lose her in the kitchen."

I blushed. Why did I always blush? "It's all right, Anna, I'm going anyway. I'll get the bus."

"Right then, I'll ring you over the weekend, Lyn, and keep you informed. Cheers!" Anna left, and the kitchen seemed full of silence.

We both sat, separated by a great length of table, and by something else . . .

"I'm sorry, Mr Baxter."

"You're sorry? Why should you be sorry?"

"For getting lost, and all." I couldn't look at him. I was determined to stay cool.

"Oh, come off it, Lyn; it wasn't your fault. If you hadn't been taken ill you might have got back quite safely."

There was a pause, which was filled, for me at any rate, by the thought of Featherbed Moss; the slimy, shifting bog that was between me and Tarn House that night. I shivered, stood up, and began collecting mugs.

"Funny, I always think of you on that course, in the kitchen. You spent a lot of time in the kitchen."

"Skiving, actually," I admitted as I passed him on my way to the sink.

"I knew that; yet you didn't find the work too hard, did you?"

"I was just too tired to think. Skivvying was all I was up to; skivvying and skiving." I laughed, nervously, at the feeble joke and ran the hot tap. The water came out cold. "I was going to clear this lot up," I said, making a lot of clatter to cover my feelings. What feelings? I daren't think.

"Julia will be here any minute. She'll lend me the Mini and I'll run you home."

I could just imagine the comments if our Kev was in when I rolled up in a car with Soupy. But before I could protest the door opened and a woman came into the kitchen. She was very tall, very thin, and she looked very tired.

"Hello, Roger. Doing a bit of private tuition?" She smiled across at me. She had a thin, wide mouth with no lipstick. Her face was lined and scrubbed clean, devoid of make-up.

"Julia – this is Lyn," Soupy announced.

"Ah, Lyn. The famous one, are you?"

"I don't know about that," I said. Something about her made me smile; her eyes looked right at me, as if concentrating on my every word. She didn't move about the kitchen doing things as she talked, like my mother would have. She just leaned on the table and looked at me.

"Oh, I know about it right enough. You've had a bad time, Lyn. It must have thrown you right off balance. Poor you."

I didn't know what to say. Do I ever? I was embarrassed, but, in a funny way, relieved to have the diabetes mentioned by a stranger.

"I'm getting the hang of the balancing, now, so I feel a lot better," I said, surprised that I really did.

"That's very positive anyway. Have you come to see Anna? I don't think she's here." Julia looked about her vaguely, as if she'd lost a hankie, not a daughter.

"She has been," Soupy explained. And he told her about my suspension.

Julia opened her pale eyes very wide and clucked at me in sympathy. "Well, one more week's rest won't do you any harm, I'm sure." She smiled, as if consoling me for missing a treat. At least there was one person who agreed with me.

But Soupy had done his negotiating while I was basking in Julia's comfort.

"Come on, Lyn," he said briskly, sounding more like a teacher than usual. I came to with a jump and slung my bag on to my shoulder.

"'Bye, Lyn." Julia was still looking at me, smiling at me. I was struck again by her exhaustion. "Call any time."

"Thanks, Mrs Hitchens, I'd like to." I raised a hand and beamed at her, then followed Soupy out of the back door.

"Somebody should have done all that washing-up," I said to Soupy as he backed the Mini down the steep drive. "She looked done-in."

"Skivvying again, Lyn?" Soupy teased. "Don't worry, Adrian will sort out the kitchen."

"Is she the cleaner?"

"He is an actor who works his passage."

I stood corrected, and thought about the Hitchens' peculiar household.

"Is Mr Hitchens a professor?" I asked.

"He was a lecturer; my tutor, actually."

"Was? He can't have been made redundant, surely?"

"He died last year."

I shut up. Oh, Lyn Bugge, you're always so full of your own troubles, aren't you? I thought of Julia. Poor, poor, Julia, who looked so exhausted, who gave me such comfort, whose husband was dead.

And Anna, whom I'd always thought of as full-of-herself, a bit spoiled maybe, with a doting father in the background, not exactly rich, but comfortable . . . comfortable. No wonder she kept herself so busy.

"Here you are, then." Soupy broke into my thoughts and pulled up at the kerb. Here I was, outside our house, on the estate a few miles away from Anna's house. A world away.

"Thanks for the lift, Sou . . . Mr Baxter." I tried to open the door, but it wouldn't budge.

"Roger," he said, leaning across to release the catch. "If we're fighting on the same side, we may as well be on first-name terms. And Lyn, I wondered whether you'd like to come out on the hills, one day, away from all the hassle? No A-level Geog, I promise." And he grinned, looking all of twelve.

Would I? Oh would I not! But should I? What about teachers and pupils and all that stuff?

"A few of us are going on Monday, when the Peak is quiet."

Ahh, so it wasn't going to be just the two of us. Well, that was all right. Wasn't it?

"Er . . . yes . . . thanks . . . I'd like that."

"Good. As you're on the route we'll pick you up about

ten. Regards to your dad when he comes home. Tell him to give me a ring if there's any problem – at Julia's."

"Yes, I will, thanks . . . and for all your help . . ."

"No trouble – no thanks needed. And don't worry about the suspension. It's not really that, you know. Just to let things cool a bit. Maybe all for the best."

And he patted my shoulder and smiled right at me. I thought I'd be too weak to get out of the car. I floated up the pathway and into the empty – thank goodness – house. Then as I drifted upstairs, I caught a glimpse of myself in the mirror and saw the stupid smile all over my face.

Chapter 9

Trundle, trundle, rattle rattle, swoosh. Trundle, trundle, rattle rattle, swoosh. Trundle . . .

I lay in bed in a soggy, sweaty mess listening to the rhythm of the washing machine. Mental note number one – ask Dr Ransome to sort out my miserable mornings. I pulled a hankie from under my pillow and mopped my sweaty hair.

It sounded as if Kev was having a laundry festival downstairs. Kev was always the one to sort out the washing; he kept the whole family in clean underwear. But why do it on a Saturday, the one day when Mam and me could have a lie-in?

Well, not the only day, not now, not for me.

I groaned and thought about the mess at the College. I hadn't told anybody at home. I had hardly seen anybody at home. Mam was out all evening – never even came in for her tea. Kev cooked cheese toasties and we watched 'Neighbours' and then he went out, giving me all sorts of instructions about my injections and my supper.

He was right, too. This was the first morning I'd woken

feeling almost human. I listened hard, trying to trace the movements of the family, over the noise of the machine. If I did an injection right now somebody would be bound to barge in.

Mental note number two: make a 'Keep Out' sign for my door. As if reading my mental notes, somebody knocked and waited. Perhaps it was late... perhaps it was Dad already. I pushed myself further up on the pillow and tried to grin. I yawned enormously. My mouth felt as if I'd been sucking pennies all night.

"Come in," I said.

She was all dressed up – very dressed up: trench-coat, silk throw, patent pumps, opaque black tights. Her dark hair hung straight and glossy, her face was creamy-smooth.

"I thought you might need a drink to get you going," Mam announced.

"You look as if you're already going," I observed.

"I'm just nipping into town." A bit defensive, that.

"Has Dad arrived?"

A blank look came over her eyes, like a blind dropped over a window. "Later, I expect," she said. She put the tray on my dressing-table, pushing aside the Dram Soc file as she did so.

"Is this yours?" she asked in her bright, interested voice.

"Mmmm." I made it sound dead boring. In fact, I was excited about the sketch I'd written last night. That interview with Cleaver had given me new insight into the idea of satire.

"What's in it?"

"Just a few bits for the Rag Revue."

"Are you acting in it?" God, she was so ambitious.

"No, just sorting out a few jokes and such-like."

To prevent further questions I started in on the coffee.

"I can take coffee without sugar, now," I reminded her. I reached out for the lumps. They were wrapped in twos in dark brown paper. "Posh," I said, turning the packet over. "Where d'you pinch these?"

"Oh, they come round with the coffee tray at meetings. I always collect mine." She looked a bit pink. "Take them for emergencies, if you like."

I dunked a digestive and slurped my coffee. Mam stirred. "Well, I'll just get off to the bus. You can do a snack for lunch and I'll bring in something for tea. All right?"

She sounded distant, as if lunch was nothing to do with her. I watched her watching herself in the dressing-table mirror; pressing her lips together, opening her eyes wide, as if getting her face ready for something. When she lifted the corners of her mouth up, she reminded me of somebody; somebody in that mirror, quite recently.

"Don't forget the washing then," she said. "Kev's out. 'Bye . . . see you later."

I looked again at the mirror, her reflection now gone. Who did she remind me of, when she smiled at herself in that mirror? I scrabbled across the bed and peered at my reflection. I flattened down my fuzzy hair, licked my lips to gloss them, and lifted them up at the corners.

Yesterday. I had that silly grin on my face after Soupy had brought me home. That was it! What had been a silly grin on me became a secret sort of smile on her. I looked again in the mirror; this time I thought about Soupy, about our journey home, our date on Monday. I groped under the bed for my glasses and looked into the mirror again.

There it was, her smile. Who would have thought we two shared anything? Well, we did now.

But if my silly grin was on account of Soupy, who caused hers?

As I took a blood test (high, of course), a urine test

(another high) and sorted out the insulin from the fridge, I thought about that smile. Why should we share it? Mam was a family legend for being the odd one out. There was Dad and Kev and even Gran, all fair-haired, pink skin and blue eyes, and I had gingery frizz, pale skin and freckles. Nobody but Mam had deep, dark eyes and straight, heavy hair. And yet . . . there was that smile. Could a smile be hereditary? If this damned disease could be, anything could.

I cleared up the needle and the empty bottles and thought enviously of the kits they'd showed me at the clinic: an injector like an ordinary pen filled with insulin cartridges; computerised blood-monitors nestling in their slim plastic boxes no bigger than a Walkman; nifty lancets, all packed into a neat leather bag. No fiddly little bottles, no disposable syringes, just a lot of money; given about £300, I knew better things to spend it on than diabetic gadgets. Like an electronic typewriter.

I collected all the bits and put them in my bin. As I pulled the quilt off the bed, I heard something drop on the carpet. It was Mam's sugar. I picked it up and now I had my glasses on I could read the lettering on it.

'The Bistro, 101 Eccleshall Road, tel.667984.'

Funny place for a council meeting.

It was dinner-time when Dad arrived, not tea-time as foretold by Gran.

"Hello, luv," he said when I staggered into the kitchen with a basket of damp washing off the line.

"Dad! Hey – you're early."

"Aye, well, I got a lift as far as top roundabout."

We stood in the kitchen grinning at each other. I clutched on to the washing basket as if I was hugging it, hugging him. But we never did nowadays. Then the phone rang.

It didn't stop ringing for the next hour. Neither did the

door bell; reporters were camping on the doorstep. Anna had started her campaign all right.

"What's to do then?" asked Dad, between answering the phone and the doorbell. When I told him about the suspension, he looked serious, and took the phone off the hook. "Does your mam know?"

"No."

"She might be able to do something."

"I don't want anything done. It's only for a week, until after the inquiry."

"Well, we can't go on living with this lot, can we?" He jerked his head out front.

"What shall we do?"

"I don't know. If your mother was here, she'd soon sort them out. Where is she?"

"In town." Lunching at The Bistro? Who with? I asked myself.

"Working?" Mam had to work some Saturday mornings, but we both knew this wasn't one of them.

"She said to get a snack – shall I do us a great late breakfast?" I only offered as a joke; Dad's a far better cook than I am.

"Aye, you do that and I'll go out and see if I can't get rid of them reporters."

I was impressed. I mean, a month ago he wouldn't have opened the door to the milkman if he could have avoided it. As I grilled the bacon and sausages, I heard the buzz of questions, and Dad's flat, calm voice going on and on. I grinned to myself; it was a technique he'd learned from his Union days: if you can't beat 'em wear 'em out.

"That's satisfied them, any road," he said as he came back.

"What did you say?" I was up to the eggs now and they were splattering in the hot oil.

"Not a lot," he lied. "Here, give us 'old, you'll ruin them eggs."

Dad was flat out on the settee and I was filling up the kitchen bin with satire when Mam and Kev appeared. Together – how'd they managed that? – they were carrying two Sainsbury's carriers each and had a sort of Christmassy air about them; giggly and noisy. I wondered if they'd been drinking.

"Hello, luv," Dad said.

"Hello, Gordon. Had a good week?" She sounded more polite than interested.

"I have that." He didn't elaborate and she didn't encourage him. She just pulled the evening paper out of her bag and waved it at me. "Quite the little activist, aren't you?" she said. "Why didn't you tell me?" Oh God! she was off again on the promoting Lyn theme.

"You weren't here," I reminded her. And she blushed.

Kev put the kettle on. "It's past four, our Lyn," he reminded me. "Have you . . .?"

"No I haven't. Just going to." I pulled a face at him.

"Wait!" ordered Mam, in her best councillor manner. I waited. She reached into one of the carrier bags. "You might find this useful," she said, handing me a parcel.

My hands started to shake; I hate getting surprises, especially in front of the family. "What's this?" I asked, though I knew. I ripped open the paper with my heart in my trainers.

It was a black bag, like those I'd seen at the clinic. I stood and looked at it. All that money! I could have had my typewriter for that.

"It's from all of us," Kev explained.

"It'll be much handier for you at college," suggested Mam, spoiling the thought as usual.

"And when you're out on the moors," grinned Dad.

I looked round at everybody. I knew nobody could really afford it. I felt embarrassed, guilty, angry . . . but not grateful.

"Thanks," I said. I didn't open the bag.

"Is that all?" our Kev asked. "Aren't you going to show it to us?"

"You mean like we used to show our scabs and scars to one another when we were kids? When am I going to get a bit of privacy in this house?" Clutching the bag, I rushed off upstairs. I could hear the explosion from Mam before I reached my bedroom. Well, what was I supposed to do? Burst into tears of gratitude? Not in front of them, I wouldn't.

Upstairs in private I wept. It wasn't out of gratitude though. It wasn't even out of self-pity; well, not entirely. It was almost out of relief. The family giving me that present was so final. It meant that my condition was now an accepted member of the family, worth investing in, with me for life. No going back, now.

I put the black bag on the dressing-table but got out my old equipment. The tests were good, in spite of my emotional state. I didn't want to go down for the insulin anyway, so I decided to leave the injection until after tea. I could hear them yattering on downstairs, obviously discussing the college business. Better I stayed out of their way. I pulled the Dram Soc file out.

I could tell what we were having for supper by the smell. Kev was doing his kedgeree – for about two hundred people judging by the mess in the kitchen. Kev's a great cook but a lousy washer-upper. I set to while he chopped boiled eggs.

"Did you use the thingy?" he asked.

"No, not yet. I haven't read all the instructions."

"I'll show you how it all works after. They gave us a demo at the surgical place."

"Thanks." I still felt embarrassed about it all, but I did want to master it before Monday's trip.

And it was really simple. Just a drop of blood on the strip, feed the strip into the meter, read the number on the screen and go man go! A pen-prick to the thigh, a shot of insulin into the system. And . . .

"Hey presto!" said Kev, withdrawing the needle from an orange with a flourish. He was really good at it. But then, it was easy to do it on an orange.

"I'm sorry you didn't like your present more," said Mam as we sat with our coffee later on. Kev had gone off with the lads, Dad to his mother's, and I had an awful feeling Mam was in one of her 'facing up to it' moods.

"I didn't say I didn't like it," I answered.

"No, but you hardly said you did, either."

"It was just such a surprise . . . a shock . . . I didn't know what to say."

"No, there's times when words won't come," she agreed, looking deep into her coffee mug.

I was puzzled; she always had the right words, for everybody else, at least.

"You seem to have had your little say up at the college yesterday," she went on, more her old self.

"Oh, Mam, I couldn't help it. It all sort of happened. I'd no idea . . ."

"The trouble with you is you never do have any idea what's going on. You need to be more aware of what's being plotted around you." She was off again, politics as usual. I gave up listening and planned some more satirical jokes for the revue.

"Roslyn, are you listening to me?" She called me to

attention. "I shall make sure that you're called to give evidence at the inquiry," she finished up.

I looked straight at her. "What for?" I asked.

"Because the whole thing was triggered off by you; because you are the only one who can tell what it was like; because you owe it to Baxter, and because . . ."

"Because you'd like me to be politically active?"

"Everybody should be politically active in a democracy."

I knew the words so well that I was mouthing them along as she said them. I felt suddenly very tired; tired of trying to live down Mam's aspirations, tired of trying to live up to Anna's, tired of the whole sickening affair.

"I'm going up," I said.

"What, already? I thought we might have a really good talk about things."

"I'm too tired."

She looked closely at me, quite concerned. Then she said, "Roslyn, I do hope you're not going to use this condition to hide behind."

Typical. Not 'have an early night,' or 'have you taken your insulin?' Just a bit of her usual pseudo-psychological counselling.

"I'm not the one in this family who hides behind things," I said.

"What do you mean?"

Actually, I wasn't sure what I meant. But whatever I meant, she took it to mean something different.

"I'm not hiding anything," she said, looking flushed and about twenty-two. "I'm just waiting for your dad to get sorted out, then we can all face up to things."

Face up to things. There's no stopping our Mam!

Chapter 10

There was certainly no stopping her on Sunday. Sunday's the day when Gran comes in to feed us with grey roast meat, long-boiled greens and lumpy mash. For the first time, I was glad I had to count the grams. Luckily, Kev's speciality is Yorkshire pud, which is so good that we eat it on its own with thick gravy, as a starter. It just about finished me, and I was wondering how to get away from the kitchen table when the phone rang.

"Lyn? I must see you. Can I come over?" It was Anna.

"We're just having dinner. Aren't you?"

"Lord no, I've only just got in from the hospital. Look, I'll get a snack and then come over. All right?"

I didn't want her to. I knew that when she and Mam got together there'd be no stopping them. Two of a kind they were.

"Lyn? Are you there?"

"Yeah . . . er . . . see you, then." I never did like Sunday dinner.

Anna talked about the student campaign. Mam talked

about the governors. Dad sat and listened and didn't say much, but at least he didn't sneak away like he used to when anyone called. Gran got on with the washing-up and Kev brought in some tea. We sat around our front room as if we were watching telly. Only it was even more boring.

"So starting tomorrow, Radio Sheaf will be doing features on the case at regular intervals; the local papers will be bombarded with letters and we think we've got a spot on local TV." Anna beamed over at me as if offering me a treat.

"What I don't understand," said Dad, surprising everybody except Anna, "is why you students are mekking all the running. 'Asn't Mester Baxter got a Union?"

"Sure, but we're fighting on much broader grounds. Cleaver and his cronies have been after the Humanities Department for years; they want to expand office technology at the expense of literature, sociology and such. It will give them great pleasure – and a bit of profit – to lose a humanities lecturer without having to pay him."

I hid my face in my mug. It was the first time I'd realised that Roger might lose his job and his salary. And all because of me and this damned condition.

"What about the Education Committee?" asked Mam.

"They won't even talk to us."

"They will to me," said Mam, grimly. "I'll be in to see the Chair first thing tomorrow. I'm going to insist she calls our Lyn to appear at the inquiry."

There was a pause. Anna bit into her umpteenth biscuit and spooned more sugar into her tea. I felt Kev wince as he watched, and I knew he was wondering whether I'd done all my routine properly. Thanks to the new gadget I'd done it all very easily. Thanks to the early night and late injection, I'd actually felt much better. Till now.

"How d'you feel about that?" Dad spoke to me.

"Mmmm, not keen . . ." I mumbled.

"Not keen's your motto!" Mam laughed. "You were 'not keen' on going on to college, 'not keen' on taking A-levels." She turned to Anna. "I sometimes wonder if there's anything she is keen on."

Anna smiled sympathetically, managing to take in Mam's impatience and my embarrassment at the same time. She'd make a good GP.

More pause. I knew what I *was* keen on: being cured. That was really the only thing that mattered to me just then. Only I daren't say that.

"If I thought it'd be any use, I'd do it," I said. "But I've made a written statement which they'll use. And I have been asked to keep away for a week."

"Exactly," said Anna, mysteriously.

"Well, that's all right then," I said.

"All right for you, our Lyn, but what about next time they want to get rid of somebody – student or teacher. Don't you ever think about other people?" I've heard Mam saying that all my life: the starving millions, the homeless, the crippled. Give her a cause and she'd devote the whole family to it, whether we wanted to be involved or not.

Pause . . . pause . . . pause . . . Anna crunched her ginger-nut; Kev slurped his tea; Dad sighed; Mam snorted. I glared round at the lot of them.

"You see, Lyn," explained Anna, as if I was six, "they've set a precedent, suspending you like that. They gave you no fair warning, no notice, they didn't go through the channels agreed with College Council and the Students' Union. They'd use suspension like schools use detention if we didn't fight them all the way."

"There was no reason to suspend you, to deprive you of your education," said Mam. "You have every right to fight."

"I don't want to fight," I said. And dammit, those stupid

tears collected again. "I'm not going to become one of your causes – either of you – if you want to tackle the whole educational system you can do it without my help." Then I stopped to breathe deeply and to gulp. Kev, squashed onto the pouffe at my feet, gave my ankle a little squeeze in sympathy. I wished he wouldn't and rummaged for my hankie.

Dad held his out to me. "If you don't want to face this tribunal, you don't have to," he said calmly. "Now don't upset yourself."

"Nay, our Mam," Kev agreed, "you know she shouldn't be upset." Kev, standing up to our Mam. I was so gobsmacked that the tears stopped.

"I'm not upset," I said, contrarywise. "I just need to be left alone, a bit of time . . . space . . ."

"You've got till Thursday," offered Mam. "Just think on." And she collected up all the tea mugs and clattered out with them. Any other time Kev and I would have laughed at her attempt at housewifery.

"I must go," said Anna, uncurling her long legs from our low settee. "Look, I have the legal advisers to the union coming to see me tomorrow morning. Come and meet them – at home, not in college."

"No, I'm . . . er . . . busy tomorrow." They all looked great question-marks at me. "I'm hiking out on the tops," I said.

"By yerself?" exclaimed our Kev. "Eeh, our Lyn, I don't think you should."

"Why not, you're all always telling me how normal I am, how I ought to live a normal life, how I mustn't hide behind my disability." I threw this last one out at Mam in the kitchen. "And anyhow, I shan't be on my own."

"Oh, you're going with Roger and his ramblers," Anna said. "She'll be all right with them," she reassured Kev.

"She wasn't all right last time she was out with him," he muttered.

"Kev!" I was embarrassed.

". . . when she was out with all of us," Anna reminded him. "It was nobody's fault, you know."

"I shall know, come Thursday." Then he stood up, looking small and fat and crumpled at the side of Anna, whose long straight hair and long straight legs were both pale, smooth, immaculate.

"Well . . . er . . . thanks for the tea, Kev . . . Mr Bugge . . ." Anna made a move. "'Bye, Pam," she called to the kitchen. I couldn't think who she meant until Mam appeared.

"'Bye, Anna. Keep up the good work," she said. And they smiled to each other: scions of the secret sisterhood.

The curtain twitchers were out along the crescent as I clambered into the Land Rover next morning. I wished I'd arranged to be picked up at the roundabout.

But it was great to be out away from the city. It was a bright, windy day, with great clouds scudding over, making shadows along the fells. The bracken was sandy-coloured and dry and down in the valley the last of the leaves were whirled up in the wind.

We did about five miles and then stopped for a breather. I was pleased to see that I kept up quite well, and that Roger made no fuss about my condition . . . or anything. The rest of the group seemed to be students, friends of Soupy's I supposed, from his University days. Nobody from the college, thank goodness.

When we stopped I chewed a strip of Stymorol, leaned on a dry-stone wall and looked out at never-ending space. No wonder Dad was getting better out here.

"Unhappy memories?" Soupy came and stood at my back.

"What . . . oh no, I wasn't even thinking of last time."

"What were you thinking?"

"About me dad."

He nodded. "Yes, it'll do him good."

"It's the best thing that's ever happened to him," I said. "And we have you to thank for that."

"No, you don't. You have your . . . accident to thank for that."

"Aye, well, it's an ill wind . . ."

"Eeh bah guum, it is that," said Soupy in a terrible accent. "Here." He thrust a little packet at me. It was diabetic chocolate; a present from Soupy to me. Wow! "Keep you going without spoiling the balance," he explained. "Come on, another three miles to the pub for lunch."

But there wasn't any lunch. As it was a Monday, and winter, the pub wasn't doing food. Everybody groaned, but Roger looked worried.

"What are we going to do about you?" he asked anxiously. "You can't spend a day walking without food."

"Ah-ha!" I said. "I'm learning fast." And I produced a packet of sandwiches, crisps, nuts-and-raisins and three apples from my rucksack. "And you can have a share, if you like," I offered. A few other sensible types had sandwiches so we all shared them together round the pub table and Roger let me share his Guinness.

"Gran used to give it us in a wine-glass, after measles and mumps when we were kids," I said, pulling a face at the bitter, black stuff. "I never liked it then, and I don't like it now."

He knocked the rest back and beamed. "Good stuff that," he said. "But you're better off without it. Have another Diet Coke?"

While the others were having more drinks, I slipped off to

the lav and performed miracles with the gadget. Actually, just as Doctor Ransome had said, the readings were good because of the exercise. When I came back, Roger was on his own.

"They all wanted to go down into the village," he explained. "They'll meet up with us across the moor." And he led the way through a gap in the wall and on to the hillside.

We walked for a while without speaking. I like that, up on the moors, just plodding step after step alongside somebody you like, having no need to say anything.

Only there was a need, really. There was so much needed sorting out; I still hadn't decided whether to appear on Thursday or not. On Sunday, hassled by Mam and Anna, I was sure I was not going to be there. Now I wasn't sure any longer. I knew I ought to discuss it with Soupy - er - Roger, only I didn't know how to start. I stretched my little legs to match his steps.

"Am I going too fast?" he asked.

I grinned. "Gerroff, sir!"

He winced. "Oh, don't remind me!"

"Sorry.. er.. sorry... I just meant I can keep up with the best now..." Why does even the most casual conversation have to turn into a drama when I speak? It's not as if I haven't had plenty of practice in avoiding issues. In our family we do it all the time. Witness the fact that nobody ever discussed Dad's... breakdown. There, that's the first time I've even said the word even to myself. That's what he had, a breakdown. But nobody called it that.

"He's not himself today." That was the nearest Gran ever got to admitting Dad was ill.

"Your dad can't go," was Mum's reason for sending Kev or me to the shops. And we knew better than to ask why.

I was just as bad; I greeted him every afternoon when I

came home, just as if he'd finished a shift at the foundry. "Hello, is me tea ready?" If he was having a specially bad day he wouldn't answer and there'd be no tea, so I'd bring him a cup. That was all I could give him, a cup of tea and perhaps a vague slap on the shoulder in place of a kiss.

Soupy slapped me on the shoulder now. "I'm glad to see you so much better, this time out," he said. "You seem to be coping very well."

I couldn't think of an answer; I just nodded dumbly.

That's what I envied about Anna; her talent for talking. No, that's not what I mean; there was enough talking going on in our family all the time, it was just that we never said the important things. Anna did; she got to the heart of things when she spoke, and she was never embarrassed about your feelings - or about hers.

"So how are you feeling now?" asked Soupy.

No point in nodding. Had to answer. Feeling? If only I could tell him.

"Oh, you know," I said, shrugging off the feel of his hand where he'd slapped my shoulder.

"No, I don't," he corrected. "You tell me."

And I did. I amazed myself, but for the first time since the damned diabetes had been diagnosed, I was able to tell somebody how it felt. About the sweaty nights, the awful mornings, the perpetual worry about being balanced, about the fears for the future. I'd never talked like this to anyone before. Why should it be Soupy?

"That's what gets me down," I said. "It's going to be there, every morning for ever and ever, as long as I live. I can't bear to think about it."

"Then don't," said Roger.

"Easy said," I said.

"Easy done," he said. "Now that you've got the knack, the routine and the balanced diet, you'll hardly ever have to think about it. It must become as automatic as cleaning your teeth every morning. Or shaving," he added.

"I don't shave."

"Well, there you are then. While I'm shaving in the morning, you're doing your tests and your injection. Same time, similar place, different chore." He grinned down at me now, his hair all wild in the wind, and his lean face pink. I suddenly felt daft with happiness.

"Anna thinks I should appear at the hearing on Thursday," I said.

"I know."

"My mam thinks so too."

"And you?"

I sighed. "Not keen," I said, honestly for once.

"Then don't appear."

"You make everything sound so simple, you do," I complained.

"Everything is never simple," he said. "But you can simplify it by taking decisions and sticking to them."

"That's not easy," I said.

"I didn't say it was easy."

"Well, would it help you if I did appear?"

"I don't know, Lyn." This time he sighed. "But I do know that the decision is yours; you mustn't do it because Anna persuades you, or your mother orders you, or because you feel sorry for me. Just do it if you feel it's the right thing to do. If not, don't."

Wheew! I wasn't sure I was ready for that sort of responsibility yet. I was hoping that they'd refuse to call me. Whoever 'they' were. That would settle everything – except Mam and Anna, of course.

"There is something you could do to help," said Soupy suddenly.

"What?" I was very cautious.

"Put a bit of a spurt on, or else we'll miss the others and our transport back." He grinned and held out a hand to pull me along. When we joined the others they were all busy planning some expedition to a volcano. I didn't hear all the talk, because of the wind, but I did notice how enthusiastically Soupy joined in. It seemed he was a bit of an explorer, as well as a teacher.

"Well, if things go wrong on Thursday, you'll be free to join us," somebody said.

"If things go wrong on Thursday, I won't even have the money to get to Iceland on a Cook's tour," he replied.

I plodded on, thinking about Soupy's job. I had thought he'd just get an official telling-off, and he could take that all right. But if he lost his job! I'd seen enough of the unemployed in our own family to realise what that could mean. Even teachers were finding it hard enough to get jobs in the north just then.

I sat quiet in the Land Rover all the way home. Nobody said much; it had been a good walk. The driver came round our roundabout and I called out for him to stop.

"This'll do," I said, at the end of our street. I struggled to get out, but Soupy was there before me and held out his arms for me to jump down. I jumped.

"Thanks, sir . . . er . . ." I said, with my usual command of the language.

"Och, Lyn, I've told you my name," he said. "Now, no more blathering wi' sirs and Soupys – d'ye ken?" He shook my shoulders.

"Aye – yes, I mean, I agree . . . and Roger?"

"Aye?"

"I'll be there on Thursday."

"If that's your decision Lyn, thanks. I'll be glad to know you're there even if they don't call you."

"'Bye . . . Roger!"

'"Bye, Lyn."

I walked backwards, waving, as the Land Rover went round the island again. Well, I'd done it now. I'd actually made a decision!

Chapter 11

Have you ever noticed how history overtakes you? You spend months drooling over something: disc, frock, lad, Mountain Bike, whatever. Then just when you've scraped up the money or the courage, your life shifts; you don't need that any more. After all the saving, effort, tears, you realise you needn't have bothered.

"You're wanted over at the Town Hall," Kev told me next morning.

After the exercise on the tops and the exercise in my mind, I felt so terrific that I'd been up since eight, working on a re-write of the Comic Cuts.

"How about Colin the Ripton Ripoff and his little Cleaver?" I asked Kev.

"For what?"

"For the Rag Revue. Or d'you think I'll get suspended again?"

"No, I think you'll get done by the college feminists."

"Oh God, it's hard being a satirical writer, you're

bound to upset somebody . . ." I laughed. A bit too much.

Kev looked at me suspiciously. "You feeling all right?"

"Oh, Kev, I feel marvellous. So much better I might even be cured."

"Well, tek it steady, tha knoaws." Sometimes our Kev is more like Gran than he likes to think. "Message was from Mam," he went on. "She says you've got to be at the Town Hall at half past eleven. Something about a statement."

I groaned. Why wouldn't she let things be? Why wouldn't she let me alone? "Ring her back and tell her I'm busy," I suggested.

"I bet you daren't ring her yourself and tell her that."

He was right. We'd been brought up never to ring Mam at the office; she didn't like mixing family and work.

"Oh hell! The one day when I really feel like working, I have to go faffing about at the Town Hall."

"It might be important," he said.

"Who for?" I asked. "For Mam's votes? For Anna's CV?"

"For you," he said. "Or for your Mr Baxter."

"He's not my Mr Baxter."

"Isn't he? I thought he might be judging from the way you came back from your hike yesterday. Din't need your Doc's; walking up in the air, you were."

I stared at him. There's not much gets past our Kev. "Don't be so daft," I told him. "He's a teacher."

"Not now he isn't. Nor likely to be if you don't get down there."

"You don't care about this enquiry," I said. "It's just that Mam said jump and you think everybody's got to jump!"

"Aye, well, if you jump fast you'll just get the ten past bus."

"I don't need the bus," I said, jumping up though. "I'll bike it." So I grabbed my denim jacket and pushed off. My first mistake that morning. I could see Kev dancing up and down the causeway as I turned into the main road. I grinned to myself. I'd pinched his lovely racer instead of my rubbish one.

Mam was waiting for me outside the Town Hall. "Right, we'll go straight in, then," she said leading the way up the steps. Not even a greeting, an explanation, a thanks for coming.

"Where shall I put the bike?" I asked.

She pointed to the cycle-stands by the door.

"I haven't got the lock," I said.

"Oh, Roslyn, why didn't you come on the bus?" She always says my name like that when she's irritated.

"I'd have been late," I said.

"Oh . . . bring it up here, we'll have to leave it in the caretaker's room."

Feeling a bit daft, I carried the bike up the Town Hall steps and wheeled it across the marble floor.

"Where are we going?" I asked as she hustled me into the lift.

"We're going to make a statement," she said.

"I've already . . ."

"Yes, but that was in hospital and it was for the police. You've never made a statement specially for the hearing."

"It'll only be the same one," I muttered.

She stopped and looked hard at me. I was suddenly conscious of my thread-bare jeans and grubby sweat-shirt. She, of course, was power-dressed as usual.

"It won't be the same one; circumstances have changed, you have changed," she said. "Surely even you can understand that?"

Actually I didn't quite. But I daren't say so.

"Now listen," she went on. I could feel her wanting to shake me. "They wouldn't agree to call you at the hearing, but they did agree to this meeting. You said you weren't willing to appear on Thursday, the least you can do is to make a new statement now."

There was no answer to that. As usual she had won.

I nearly turned and ran though when we went into the office. There was Ms Patten, of course; I wasn't surprised to see her. Anna had told me she was arranging the inquiry. But she was with smoothy-chops himself, Mr Chairman Cleaver, he of the suspension order.

Ms Patten looked up. "Hello, Lyn. Feeling better by now?" I just nodded. "Good. Now, you know Mr Cleaver, I think?" Oh yes, I knew him. He smiled at me; I stared at him. She turned to the man on her other side. "Mr Carter, from our legal department, will take your statement. Now if we all sit round the table. It won't take long. Mrs Bugge?" She waved us into a couple of chairs opposite.

When we had settled ourselves their legal bloke switched on a tape-recorder. "Can you recount the events of October 23rd? Just tell it as it happened. Don't worry if you need time to think, or a break. We'll just listen."

Silence. I could even hear the slight scrape as the cassette turned in the recorder. I watched it, fascinated. I said nothing.

"Lyn?" Mam prompted me, gently.

So I started.

It was the same story, but it came out differently. For once I thought carefully before speaking. Every word became a footstep on that last walk; every sentence traced my route – and my responsibility. I didn't lie; I merely told the whole story without once mentioning Sou . . . Roger.

When I finished there was silence for a moment.

"Thank you, Lyn," said Mr Carter. "That's just what we need." And he picked up his machine and disappeared through a door in the panelling.

It was as if he had taken a magic spell off me. What did he mean that was just what they needed? Who needed it? Whose side was he on anyway? I remembered Anna's words: "an *enfant sauvage*," she'd called me. Not savage, merely stupid. Mam was always telling me I'd no political awareness. I turned to look at her. For a moment she nodded reassuringly but she was soon down to business again.

"Right," she said to Ms Patten, in her best committee style. "Now you've got what you want, perhaps we can get down to what we want."

Ms Patten looked surprised. "What you want?" she asked.

"Yes. Like wanting an education for my daughter. Why is she suspended from college this week?"

"She's not suspended. She's convalescing," put in Mr Smoothy-Cleaver.

"As she's not ill, she can hardly be convalescing. She's perfectly fit enough to be back now."

"We thought, perhaps, with all the added strain, another week . . . get the hearing out of the way . . ."

"Get her out of the way, you mean. You have no right to suspend her. You've not gone through the correct procedure."

"I have not suspended Lyn. I merely advised her to stay away until things quietend down. For her own good."

"For the college's good. I think I can be the judge of what is for my daughter's good. It will do her good to get back to college, to get back to normal."

Oh if I could, if I could!

They went on and on. Mam's just like a Jack Russell

terrier when she's after somebody. And she was after him all right. Why? Was she doing it for Anna?

I couldn't concentrate on their words. I was still whittling away about Sou . . . Roger. Perhaps by leaving him out of my story I'd let him down? I felt my heart pounding, I was sweating and shaking.

"Are you all right, Lyn?" asked Ms Patten.

"It's hot in here," I muttered. "'Scuse me."

But even as I stood the floor came up to meet me.

So much for feeling better. When I came to I was on a sofa in a sort of surgery.

"OK now, love?" asked a young woman. "Past your insulin time, was it?"

"I should have been all right," I muttered. "I was low this morning."

"Aye, well, your mother explained there's been a bit of stress. It's amazing how it affects the balance. Here you are, have a drink and a biscuit, that'll help."

I sipped the lovely strong coffee, and dunked my biscuit. I had no idea where I was in that enormous building, but I couldn't be bothered to ask. I didn't have to.

Mam came in. "Oh, Roslyn," she said, bustling in ready to blame me as usual. "What a moment to choose! Just when I was telling them how fit you are."

"Choose? I don't choose to be in this state, do I?"

"No, of course you don't." For a moment she softened. "But if you feel yourself going, you should chew on a glucose sweet. They'll tide you over."

"I haven't got any. I didn't think . . ."

"No, you never do."

"I was perfectly fit this morning. Until you dragged me here."

"Until you cycled down, instead of taking the bus. I bet

you've had no breakfast – and what about your insulin pen? Where's that?"

"On my dressing-table."

"That's not much use now, is it?"

"Oh for goodness sake, Mam, stop nagging!" I was almost weeping with rage. Of course she was right; she always is. I should have brought all my gear and the glucose. I should get into the habit of never moving without them.

"Well, finish your coffee and relax," she said, gently for once. "They'll have to bring the statement in here for you to sign."

"Was it all right?"

"Was what all right?"

"What I said."

"Yes, of course it was all right. You were really good, Lyn. Cool, coherent – most convincing."

Wow! praise from our Mam. But I was too worried to bask in it. "Yes, but . . . I mean . . . will it help them, or us?"

She looked at me for a moment. "It'll help you, that's the most important thing."

"No, it's not. What about Sou . . . Mr Baxter's job?"

"You've done your bit for Mr Baxter. He's got a Union; let them fight for his job. You can't take that on yourself, Lyn."

"Anna has."

"No, she hasn't. Anna's having a grand time playing student politics. Good luck to her. But you've got a lot of work to shift before mocks and you need to be in college. That's your battle."

"No, that's your battle. You and that Cleaver in there. What's all that to do with me?"

"Everything. Look, Lyn, if we allow him to shelter behind this excuse of looking after your health, how often is he going to send you away? Every time you have a hypo? Or every time things get a bit awkward for him? I will not have you treated like an invalid. I will not have your condition used as an excuse to deprive you of anything."

She sounded so fierce that I stared at her. She was a bit pink and her eyes glistened.

"What are you fighting for, Mam?" I asked, genuinely interested.

"For you, you daft lass." She reached out and gripped my hand so hard it hurt. We looked right at each other, both of us flushed and tearful. We didn't speak.

"Mr Carter – with some documents to sign. Shall I let him in?" The nurse popped her head round the curtain.

Mam sighed. "Aye, let him in," she said. And she grinned at me. "Come on, our Lyn," she said. "Let's sign your masterpiece."

Chapter 12

"Don't wait tea for me," said Mam, packing me and the bike into an estate taxi. "I'll be going straight out after work."

"Another meeting?" I asked. I tried not to sound sarcastic but I felt let-down; I'm just deciding we're going to get on much better and she announces she won't be in. How could I improve my communications skills with somebody who was never there?

"I'm going to the theatre; it's the cheap preview night." She sounded defensive, as if I'd accused her of wasting money.

"Well, enjoy the play," I called as the cab pulled away. She waved me off – or was it away? Difficult to tell from the back window. But I was puzzled; she usually shared her cheap tickets with me.

By the time she got in, I was asleep. By the time I got up, she'd gone to work. P'raps that's the secret of getting along together.

*

I was more successful with Dr Ransome at the clinic next morning.

"Well, you seem to have bounced back all right," she said. I think she was quite surprised. "Feeling a little more sociable now?"

I grinned and pushed my glasses up. "Yeah, well, I'm sorry about last time. I was a bit bolshie."

She laughed. "Well, aren't we in The People's Republic of South Yorkshire?"

"Not yet, but Mam's working on it," I said, grinning up at her.

"Well, apart from your politics, are you having any problems keeping the balance?"

"Mornings are worst. I'm dreading next week when I have to be up and off to college by eight. It's as much as I can manage to get up at all, some days."

"Oh, that's simple. You just use a higher dose at night. I'll give you a different prescription for that. It's simpler than doubling up your daytime insulin, and more easily controlled. Don't forget your last portion before sleeping, too."

"Yes, I've learned that the hard way. My brother's always counting my portions and grams. He nags me all day."

"Isn't that sweet of him?" she beamed. She obviously thought Kev was an appealing little boy, not a scruffy overweight youth. "But you must get accustomed to self-checking; every meal, every snack, every drink. Your brother has set you on the right track; he seems to have studied your condition well."

That was true; I'd never even seen the BDA Youth-Pack since I'd brought it home. Our Kev must be learning it by heart.

"There you go," said Dr Ransome, tearing off a sheaf of

prescriptions from her pad. "These should last you a month, but there are a couple of extras in case you have to up your dose."

"A month?"

"Yes, you're in complete control now – with the help of your brother, of course." She smiled and looked directly at me. "Of course if you hit a bad patch, feel free to come in here any Wednesday morning."

I took the papers. "Thanks," I said. "I'm feeling so good now, I don't think you'll see me for another month."

"I hope not."

"Why, am I such a bad patient?"

"No, of course not. It's just . . ." she hesitated. "You feel good now, because you're well-balanced in all sorts of ways, as well as chemically. Keep it that way, and you'll continue to feel good. But we can't control every aspect of our lives; don't be depressed if this balance doesn't always see you through. You may find life at college more exhausting than you remember, you may hit a period of emotional stress – have you got a boy-friend?"

Pause for blushes. "Er . . . no . . ."

"Oh, I'm not going to give you a lecture on sex and the diabetic, Lyn. I might just as well ask have you got exams, an interview for a job, a family upset. Stresses affect anybody's chemistry; in a diabetic, they can affect it more."

"You mean like when I was first taken ill on the fell?"

"Yes. Tiredness turns into exhaustion, nausea to vomiting, dizziness to falling about, even blacking-out. A hypo, in fact."

"Oh yes, I remember Sister Mackenzie telling me all about that, with great relish. But surely I'm out of that now?"

"At the moment you are. But be prepared, watch out for warning signs, and take instant action. Remember, the level of insulin you need today may not be adequate tomorrow. You have to monitor it on a day-to-day basis." She flicked through my folder. "Have you been in touch with the BDA?" she asked.

"Who?"

"The British Diabetic Association. You were given their information pack weren't you?"

"Oh that . . . yeah."

"You should read it. Apart from useful medical information, it has a magazine and news of all kinds of social activities."

There it was again, the attempt to organise my life. Well, I had no social life anyway, but I sure as hell was not going to join a lot of diabetic crocks for fun and sugar-free games.

"I've got exams, I don't have time for much socialising."

"You seem to have enjoyed quite an active social life last weekend," she smiled.

For a moment I thought she'd spied on my outing with Roger and I glared at her.

"I read all about the clashes up at the college," she said.

"Oh . . . that." I actually laughed with relief. "That was just accidental. I'm not an activist."

"Well, you're taking a much more positive attitude to the diabetes now. Keep that in balance and the rest will follow." She held out her thin white hand to me. "A month then."

After the clinic, I felt at a loose end, like you do after exams or the end of term at school. I was full of energy, ready for anything, except solitary revision. I even wished I could have gone into college but I daren't risk it, not with the hearing tomorrow. I didn't want to do anything to cause more upsets for Roger Baxter.

The thought of him sent another surge of energy through

me. I felt elated, excited . . . I went down the windy drive, past the same queues, possibly the same people, as I'd seen last time. But now I had no need of a lift from Anna or anyone else. I just ran. I ran on and on down the wide driveway to the main road.

The Northern Infirmary was way out of the city on the edge of the moors and the wind swept my hair up above my head and cut right into my ears. At the main road, I slowed down and strode out as if on a mountain hike. I felt so restless tnat I was past the bus-stop and cutting down to Chantry Park before I knew I'd decided to walk back to the city.

"Do you have a boy-friend?" Dr Ransome had asked, as so many people had asked me so many times. If I was feeling bloody-minded I'd say yes, there were some boys who were friends of mine. I've even had several friends who were girls, plus a few men and women and sundry dogs.

But 'boy-friends'? Now don't get me wrong. I'm not a rampant feminist. I'm not strong enough for that stuff. Mam would say I'm not committed enough. The trouble is, I don't really know what I am, on the sexual spectrum. Well, yes, I do; I'm a virgin. Not just sexually, but emotionally too.

Of course, even I've been to discos with school-mates, out biking with Kev and the lads, even the occasional party. But when the lights go down and the groping starts, I back off. It's nothing so high-principled as the feminist propaganda about owning your own body. I don't think my dwarfish body is that important, but whenever a lad appears to be interested in it, I get all embarrassed. When I'm being deeply kissed, I'm not in ecstasy, I'm worrying about our teeth clashing, terrified my breath smells. And though I can see what all the groping is for, I don't actually know how to grope back.

There was a story Mam told, about the yuppie-convent

girl on her first night with her Hooray-Henry. She got into bed starkers except for a pair of very expensive kid-gloves. Henry thought this was some new technique he'd missed at his Agricultural College.

"How delightful, Dinah dwarling," he said, sliding in beside her. "What are you going to do with the gloves?"

"Well, actually, I just slipped them on, 'cos Lucinda told me I'd have to touch your ghastly Thing."

We all laughed at that story, upper-class twits being a speciality of Mam's. But I always had a sneaking sympathy with Dinah. Whenever anybody passed one of those real 'meat-mags' around school, I simply couldn't believe they were meant to turn people on to anything. Not unless they wanted to become gynaecologists.

Sometimes I wonder whether I'm frigid. Then I read a chunk of a Brontë, weep all over it and think perhaps I'm not. But where would I find a Heathcliff, or a Rochester? The only men who'd ever turned me on were in books. Until now.

I skipped down a steep, narrow path that led to the main route through the park. I was still grinning to myself over that old joke of Mam's when I saw her. In the middle of Chantry Park, miles away from City Hall, with a bloke in a Volvo – Mam. I was that gobsmacked I even began to walk towards the parked car. What did I think I was going to say? "Who's yer friend, our Mam?"

I wish I dared. But of course, Super-Lyn, woman of the nineties, did just what you'd expect: she avoided the car, the issue, the problem, and trotted off down a little side-lane.

It took me up through what Gran always calls 'rodidandrons' and skirted the road where they were parked. I could see quite clearly the two people – were they a couple? – inside the big car, deep in conversation. I knew it was her; I'd recognise that heavy, shiny bob anywhere; her head seemed to rest on his shoulder, peering downwards then turning up to him. He bent to look down at her as he twisted the ignition key. Perhaps he smiled into her eyes; perhaps I only made that up; I've read my share of magazine stories.

As the car pulled away I raced down the little track, and watched it glide off towards the city. I ran along the road, unthinking. I ran until my breath gave out. Not as fit as you think I am, Dr Ransome, I thought with satisfaction. Why satisfaction? I stood there stupefied and breathless, leaning on a bus-stop. A bus approached. 'Brookes' it announced on the front, the area where Anna lived. Suddenly I didn't want to go home. I stuck out my hand and the bus pulled in. Without a thought in my head, I was on my way.

I recognised the house by the mini parked in the drive and the carved Gothic patterns round the porch. I rang, then I knocked, but there was no reply. I stood in the gaunt stone porch, listening to the wind battering a branch against the great stone side of the house. Clouds had blown up since my walk and it was quite dark behind the high grey walls. Brontëland! I had a sudden urge to get back to our squeaky-clean kitchen in our little council house. But the threatened rain started as it often does over the hills, sudden, sharp and very heavy.

I turned back and tried the door. It opened so I walked in. At first I thought the sound of knocking was from the banging branch outside, then I realised somebody was using a hammer. I followed the noise over to the left of the hall and peered into a room. I saw nobody but the steady banging continued. The room was lined with shelves of books; it could have been Anna's father's study; Anna's late father's study. I shuddered and backed away into the hall – and into a body. Somebody behind me held my shoulders – hard.

"Hello, young Lyn. What're you doing here?"

Roger Baxter's voice.

I felt faint and slightly sick. My legs wobbled as I turned to look up at him, not so much with adoration as from fright.

Before I could get up the strength to reply there was a ghostly screech from the corner.

"Hell and damnation, it's got woodworm!" Julia Hitchens emerged from behind a big leather chair. "Oh, Lyn, how lovely to see you again. I'll be back in a minute."

And she walked straight past us and disappeared through a little door at the end of the hallway.

"She won't, you know," laughed Roger. "She'll be hours." He let his hands drop from my shoulders. "You've stopped shaking now? Och, I'm afeerd I startled you. I'd thought you'd heard me."

"Nobody could hear anything with that hammering going on. I did ring but . . ."

"The bell doesna' work. And anyway the door's always open."

"So I see," I said faintly. My heart – honest – went pit-a-pat or flip-flop, or whatever words those soppy songs and stories use. I must have been more frightened than I cared to admit.

"Come in, come in," he said moving off towards the kitchen. "It's great to see you again." And he looked sideways down at me. Like Mam's bloke in the car, I thought, and fear clutched me again, like belly-ache.

"I'll make some coffee," said Roger.

Julia appeared just as the coffee was made. We sat dunking Rich Tea biscuits and talking about the hearing – of course.

"Och, I don't care which way they decide, I just want it all over," said Roger.

"Oh but you must care," Julia said. "Reputation, reputation, reputation . . ."

Roger ignored the quotation. Perhaps he didn't even recognise it. "I'm not sure that I want to make my reputation in teaching," he said.

"Nor ruin it, presumably," she added. "Look, get out of this clear, then you can decide on the teaching."

"What's wrong with teaching?" I asked.

"Have you got twenty-four hours to spare, Lyn?" Roger laughed.

Had I? For him? Had I!

"Come on, Roger," Julia was saying. "Education needs bright young folk like you. Andrew always wanted you to end up in his department."

"Andrew was a wonderful man and an inspired teacher; I'm neither."

She didn't reply, but her pale eyes sparkled as she thought of Andrew. Anna's father, presumably. She sighed, and looked quite frail. But she stood up and shook herself and beamed at us. "I must get on, I have a production meeting at two. If you want to wait for Anna, help yourself to a snack, Lyn. Roger will see to you."

She left us alone in the kitchen.

"We really must give up meeting like this," said Roger as we cleared up the pots. I looked up at him, startled. "Only a joke, Lyn," he explained. "Although, come to think of it, I'd like us to go on meeting just like this," he said in his soft Scottish accent.

Whheeeeeeew! Cor! Holy mackerel! Jumping Jehosophat! And any other such coherent exclamations.

I leant against the table for a moment, then went across the kitchen to the sink with the mugs. I ran tepid water into the bowl and rinsed them. I dared not speak. I dared not look at him.

As soon as I finished the mugs I turned to attack the breakfast things. I rubbed and I scrubbed and I rinsed and I mopped as if I was being paid piece-work rates; even Gran would have been impressed.

Roger wasn't. "There's no need," he protested. "It'll all be piled into the machine tonight."

"'I've started so I'll finish,'" I quoted just as grimly as that grim man on TV.

"Och, Lyn, you're always busily avoiding things."

"What do you mean?"

"Well, up at Tarn House, you were always the first to offer to wash up so that you could avoid the fun and games."

"I was that tired."

"You were that shy."

"Shy? Me? Why, you hardly know me!" He certainly didn't know Ladlass Lyn the dare-devil of Thornton Street Juniors.

"I think you're shy," he said, standing directly behind me. "Of me anyway." And he tugged the back of my hair very gently.

Wooow! I could feel goose-pimples right up my arms, right down my back, even under my sweater. "Well," I said huskily. "You are a teacher."

"Nobbut just," he said in Scots-Yorkshire. "This time tomorrow I may not be."

"I hope to God you still are," I gulped, feeling sickened at the thought that he might lose his job because of me. I stood in front of the sink, peering at the washing-up bubbles as if reading the tea-leaves like Aunty Edie. The house was silent except for the humming of the fridge.

He stood bending over me, his breath ruffling through my hair. "Lyn, it doesn't matter now. You mustn't blame yourself. I was in charge, responsible – or irresponsible. Me – not you." His long arms reached over and took the mop out of my hand. "And you're not to worry about it. Balance – remember?" He smiled and turned me gently. I gazed at the intricate pattern on his fair-isled chest and nodded. I felt as though I was suspended in a bubble; if I spoke it would burst. I just wanted to stand there, snug against his hairy sweater, without a thought, a care, a problem; as if there was no tomorrow – especially tomorrow.

"Will I be seeing you at the enquiry tomorrow?" he asked softly.

That burst my bubble. I leaned back on the sink and looked up at his blurred image through my misted glasses. "I'm not being called," I admitted.

"Ach, I'm well pleased about that. You've enough on without being interrogated by the Cleavers of this world."

"I've made a new statement and that's being used. I tried to make it fair, Roger."

He moved closer now; I thought for a mad moment he was going to . . . Carefully he removed my glasses, breathed on them and polished them with a tea-towel.

"I'm sure you did, Lyn," he said, placing my glasses back on my nose and threading them under my hair. "And I'll see you tomorrow after the event . . . celebrate or commiserate, eh?"

I straightened the glasses and saw him clearly. His dark hair flopped across his forehead, his deep-set eyes peered beneath with an odd expression, almost . . . well . . . shy.

"Tomorrow then," I said.

And together we finished the pots.

Chapter 13

I drifted home . . . I floated home. Actually I took two buses, but I had no memory of the journey by the time I walked up to our front door.

Before my key was in the lock, the door fell open. "Where the hell do you think you've been till now?" demanded Kev. He sounded so much like the outraged dad in one of those gritty Northern films that I giggled at him and pushed past up the stairs.

"Hallo, love." Gran's voice greeted me from the front room. "Come on in by the fire and I'll mash."

I came back down, past a glowering Kev. "Hello, Gran," I said.

"Did you have to queue all morning?" she asked me.

I looked at her blankly. I'd forgotten where I'd been.

"No, she bloody didn't," said Kev. He sounded quite fierce. "I told you, she'd left the place before eleven."

"Aahh!" I began to touch ground. "The hospital . . . how did you know what time I left?"

"I was there. I called in at the Diabetic Clinic on my way out."

I winced at the name. "What for?"

"I thought, madam, we might have a coffee, a chat, come back home together . . . whatever."

"No, I mean what were you up at the hospital for?"

"For an interview." Kev spat out the word as angrily as he'd spat at me.

"For a job?" I asked.

"No, for a pay-bed in the maternity unit." For the first time Kev's eyes twinkled, his round face glowed, not with ill-temper, but with something approaching pride.

"And?" I asked.

"And where have you been all this time?" he countered, pushing me on to the settee.

"Aw, gerrof, our Kev, and tell me all about it." I patted the cushions and he sat down beside me. He sat straight, not with his usual floppy stretch. It struck me that he looked inches taller than he ever would be.

"Now," I commanded. "Tell me all. How did you hear about the job? What is it? Did you get it? When do you start?"

"Hold on a minute. You're not an investigative journalist yet, my lass. 1. From Anna. 2. Occupational Therapy. 3. Yes. 4. Monday." He leaned back, folded his arms, and waited.

I was gobsmacked. For a moment I just stared at him; cuddly, teddy-bear, prickly old Kev, tasting success for the first time in his life. I could almost feel my sugar-level rising.

"Oh, our Kev, that's grand. I'm that pleased for you." I launched myself at him and we went into a great clinching hug. We were laughing and punching and very nearly crying together on our old settee.

"Now then, that's enough," said Gran, with the usual

Yorkshire talent for cutting off any exhibition of joy. "We'd best have some dinner."

We fell back to our separate corners, a bit ruffled, a bit embarrassed. Gran pottered off to the kitchen.

"I never knew you were interested in hospital work, Kev," I said.

"I wasn't, never even considered it until your 'do'. What with visiting you, reading all them leaflets – which you've never done, by the way – and talking to Anna."

"You've been talking to Anna?" I asked. "I thought you didn't like her."

"Whatever gave you that idea? As a matter of fact we've had the odd drink together, now and then, you know."

"I didn't know." I felt a bit let down, then. I thought of Anna as my friend, not Kev's.

"Anyway, I decided if cleaning was good enough for her, it was good enough for me. I asked her to look out for vacancies. There weren't any. Women take them all, because it's flexi-hours to fit in with kids an' all."

"Aye, women would have to do that, wouldn't they?"

"When you've finished putting in your feminist penn'orth ... She did hear of a place over in the OT print shops, sort of technician. So Anna mentioned my name. I did that printing course with YTS – you remember?"

I did remember. Another of Kev's disappointments; nothing ever came of the year he spent at the print-works. As usual, as soon as the YTS finished and he was ready to go on the pay-roll, they gave him the push and took on another YTS kid.

"This morning," he went on, "after you'd gone, the Head of OT rang and asked me to go over and have a look around."

"And?"

"And they want me." He sounded shocked that anyone would.

"Well done, that lad!" I exclaimed, banging him hard on the shoulder.

"Aye, 'an't he been a clever duck?" asked Gran. She thrust a big tin of vegetable soup at him. "Now open that and be a bit more cleverer."

We paraded into the kitchen and Gran and I stood by in admiration while Klever Kev opened the tin of soup.

Over dinner, Kev told me more about the job in the print-shop, which was part of the Occupational Therapy in the Psychiatric Section. He would be working with groups of mentally handicapped youths and their instructors. I knew that he'd enjoy keeping the machinery in order; he loved fiddling around with mechanical bits and pieces. But how would he get on with the workers? He was more sensitive than he'd ever admit.

"D'you think you'll get on with them all right?"

"Who?"

"The mentally handicapped youths."

"Why not, I get on with you all right."

I laughed and chucked a bit of bread into his soup.

"No, don't laugh. I mean it. Look, our Lyn, you have one kind of disability – now don't get all uppitty – you have to face it. You've got a bit of your body chemistry askew. Well, so have they, only it's a different bit. They are human beings, you know. They have the same interests, the same irritations, the same needs as I have." He sat back, pink and puffy after his unusually long speech.

We grinned at each other over the bowls of tepid soup. Gran has this theory that you're only allowed so much electric and she never leaves the plate on long enough for things to heat right through. When we all collapse with salmonella it won't be the cheese, the pie or the eggs, it'll be Gran's semi-cooking.

"So how did you get on up at t'hospital?" she asked me, blowing her soup even cooler.

"Fine, just fine. Everything's all right."

"Well, there y'are then," she said.

Am I? Where am I?

Up in the clouds with Roger?

Down in the dumps with Mam?

"What'd you do after?" asked Kev.

Yes, well, what did I do after? Spy on our Mam with her fella? Have an intimate moment with my teacher?

"I walked across the park then got a bus to Anna's. Had a coffee with her mother." It was true.

Kev looked relieved. Why? Did he already suspect something between me and Roger? Had he caught a glimpse of Mam in that car? I looked closely at his cherubic face.

"Anna told me that the biggest demo yet is planned for tomorrow," was all he said.

I groaned. "And the press, TV, local radio and all, I suppose?"

"Aye, I expect so. She certainly gets things moving, does Anna." He looked thoughtfully at the bit of crust he was pulling at. "She's moved a few things for me, that's certain."

I wondered about Anna and my brother. Was he yet another of her campaigns, another good deed notched up? No, that wasn't fair. She certainly could get things moving, could Anna. Like our Mam.

"Like our Mam," said Kev. And I feared for him. Poor Kev, if he didn't come a cropper over Anna, he certainly would over Mam. "Shall you join in?" he asked me.

"You know I can't go near the place." I was secretly glad

about that. My last brush with the media had left me feeling a right fool.

"You'll be better off here at home tomorrow, love," said Gran, collecting the pots. "Who's washing up?"

"Kev."

"Lyn."

We both spoke at once.

Up in my room I pulled the Drama Soc file out and re-read my not-very-funny jokes. There must be some way of capturing hospital life on paper; something better than slightly rude, ever-so-patronising jokes. I remembered a play I'd seen years ago – with Mam's cheap preview ticket – about a man paralysed from the neck down who was fighting, not for his life, but for the right to unplug his support system. Sounds morbid, I know, but it was hilariously funny. How can you be funny about dying and disability?

'Disability'. That's what I had. Could I ever be funny about diabetes? I looked at the blank paper in front of me, and thought hard about the play. I'd enjoyed it so much that I'd persuaded Kev to take me again, and I'd seen the film. I could hear some of the dialogue in my head. I picked up my pencil and started to scribble.

From several miles away, I heard Kev taking Gran home, and the house fell silent. I wrote on, page after page of dialogue. When I stopped I knew it wasn't just a funny sketch. It was a play. And it wasn't funny-funny, it was funny-furious.

I flopped back on my bed; I was whacked! It was already dark outside, so I leaned across to draw the curtains. Just before they closed, a car drew up at the end of our road, a big, dark car. Mam got out, peered inside to say something, then slammed the door and stepped out briskly along the pavement as if she'd just come up from the bus.

I suddenly felt sick. The afternoon's scribbling had made me forget the problems around me. Now, they were arriving back home. I heard Mam call out and Kev answer her from the kitchen. I didn't.

I was driven back down by the need for an injection and for my tea.

"Hello, Lyn. Been working away up there?" she said.

I walked to the fridge, collected my bottles and muttered an answer. When I came down again they were sitting by the fire.

"Oh, good – you can lay the table, our Lyn," said Kev. "I've done the tea, you can do your bit."

"Yes, all right," I agreed. He looked at me, surprised. I never do any domestic work without a fuss.

Kev had made his special stuffed pancakes. Not those things you only have on Shrove Tuesday, with oranges and sugar; these were some Italian recipe he'd picked up from a telly programme. They were rolled up and filled with spinach and creamy cheese and were absolutely delicious. I could have eaten half-a-dozen, but crafty all-watching Big Brother had only made nine. "Three's your portion, our Mam never eats much and I have to watch the podge," he said, dishing them out.

After tea we sat on round the kitchen table for a bit. I was still away with my characters in my play, and Kev and Mam nattered on about his job.

"I hear you had a good session at the clinic," she turned to me.

I nodded.

"And what about Mr Cleverclogs here, then?" she said.

I turned to Kev. "Have you told me Dad yet?" I asked, knowing the answer.

They both looked guilty, though for different reasons, I thought.

"Aw no, we'll never get through this time of night," said Kev. There was only one public phone up at the centre, and of course all the rangers wanted to contact their nearest and dearest, and perhaps even their wives, at off-peak times.

"You should have thought of that before now," I replied.

"He'll be ringing himself tomorrow," Mam put in. "You can tell him then."

I got up and started clearing – again.

"Nay, let's have a coffee by the fire and clear up after," suggested Kev. "I feel like celebrating."

"You two go and sit down, I'll clear up and make the coffee." I spoke to Kev. "Just this once, for a celebration." I couldn't face her on our own.

"Goodness me, Lyn, what's come over you all of a sudden?" She smiled. But she accepted the offer and they went to watch the C4 News while I washed up.

When I brought in the coffee Kev had flopped down on the pouffe at Mam's feet. "I did try," he said, "but the line's engaged all the time."

"Never mind, love, you've done your best," she comforted him. She stroked the back of his neck, absent-minded like, as if she was thinking of somebody else's neck. Or was I remembering somebody else's hand?

I flipped.

"You make me sick, you two. You sit there all curled up and contented while me Dad doesn't even know the biggest news we've had in the family for years."

They both looked up at me, amazed at this attack.

"What do you think he must feel like?" I raged on. "Stuck out there up the Peak, away from all of us, not knowing what's going on." And I looked directly at Mam.

"Hey, hey, calm down, our Lyn," soothed nanny Kev.

"I'll try again, if you like. Bound to get through sometime." And he poddled off in his stockinged feet to the hall.

"What did you mean?" she asked, looking steadily at me with those clear grey eyes.

"What?" I wavered.

"About your Dad, not knowing what's going on. You meant more than Kev's news, didn't you?"

I could hear the gas jets pop-popping, and Kev's foot banging a rhythm against the stairs. I felt cold, clammy; my hands, when I clenched them, were sweaty.

"I walked back from the Northern through Chantry Park," I said.

Her expression never changed. Suddenly I understood why she was so successful, so respected at work and on the council. She was really cool, was our Mam.

"Aahh . . ." was all she said.

We faced each other in silence. From a long way off, I was aware of Kev's voice, burbling on. He must have got through. Like I had.

"It's not an affair, if that's what you're thinking," she said. "It's much more important than a mere affair to me."

I couldn't speak. As usual the tears were welling, my throat ached and my breathing was unsteady and I just had to get to the lavatory. Oh, hell, how was I ever going to get through the tough bits of life if this happened every time?

"Mam!" yelled Kev. "Here's Dad for you."

Before she could get up, I rushed up the stairs to the bathroom. I was sweating buckets but I wasn't actually sick. This was progress? She was still listening to Dad, answering briefly, when I emerged. She looked up the stairs and our eyes met. She offered me the phone. I shook my head, turned into my bedroom and shut the door.

And there was still tomorrow!

Chapter 14

"Lyn . . .? Are you awake?" Mam tapped at my door. I groaned, not just because it was her, more as a general statement of my own condition. The Condition. All my fault, I knew that's what she'd say. But I just hadn't been able to face her last night, so I had neither my snack nor my night-insulin. Result – like a bad, bad hangover.

Mam came in with a tray. "Come on, Lyn, you'll feel better when you've had something to eat." She pulled back the curtains on a dark, dank day. "There's tea, biscuits and insulin on that tray and you look as though you need the lot."

I cowered under the quilt – coward! As soon as she left, I grabbed my gear and rushed to the bathroom.

I was propped up on my pillow, sipping and dunking, when she came back. I concentrated on my Rich Tea and, uninvited, she sat on my stool.

"We've got to sort one or two things out," she said.

I couldn't think of a reply.

"I know what you're thinking," she said. She couldn't; even I didn't know that.

"Aren't you going to be late?" I asked.

"I'm not going until we've had a chat, Lyn. God knows they owe me enough time at the moment."

"Yeah, you have been putting in a lot of extra hours," I agreed.

"Not in the way you think," she said sharply. "Look, I've not told anybody in the family about this . . ."

"So why tell me?"

"Because if I don't you'll go on thinking the worst and life in this house will be more intolerable than it usually is."

I was shocked. I mean, it's all right for teenagers to rebel against home-life, but you don't expect middle-aged parents to. For the first time that morning I looked at her. She was wearing her old track-suit, no make-up, and her hair looked flat and greasy. At that moment she looked all of her forty years.

"I don't know what you mean," I said.

"No, I don't think you do, Lyn."

I noted with interest that I was no longer 'Roslyn' to her. Was our Mam about to turn into My Best Friend?

She sighed, shifted on my stool and rubbed her cheeks with her fingers. "It's not been easy, these past two years, you know, with your dad . . ."

"It's not been easy for Dad."

"Of course it hasn't," she spoke softly, and looked across the room as if it was a long, long way, "not for many years. He hated the foundry, you know, always wanted to be in the fresh air, out on the fells. There never seemed any alternative, in those days; it was either the pit or the steel-works . . ."

"And now he's found an alternative," I said.

"And I'm really proud of him," she said. "Make no mistake about that."

"But?"

She shook her head and looked straight at me. I felt a confession coming on and squirmed my toes under the cover.

"I've got a place at Birkbeck College," she said.

I was gobsmacked. Not a word in me. There was I expecting a 'True Confession' and, as usual, Mam was talking education. Even I knew that Birkbeck was a college in London where mature students could study for a degree.

"Well done, you," I said, striving for irony. "Congratulations."

"Yes, well, I'm past that. The place has been open to me for over a year while I've been dithering. Now I either accept it or lose it."

I thought about that. A year ago, I was starting college, Dad was facing redundancy, Kev was unemployed and Mam was our bread-winner. So, 'There is a tide in the affairs of men,' I thought. And women, especially women.

"So what are you going to do?" I asked.

"Accept, of course." Her voice was brisk now; her usual committee-self. "Peter – the man you saw – has been a terrific help. I had to submit a paper, you know. That's why I often worked on at the office."

"You could have worked at home. Like I have to."

"Oh, Lyn, at least you have a room of your own. And I needed all the office technology: computer, word-processor . . ."

"And Peter," I added.

She actually blushed. "And Peter," she agreed, her eyes shiny, her fingers touching her face.

Watching her, I remembered Roger's fingers in my hair, yesterday. Suddenly I was flooded with the memory of him, his voice, his touch, his hairy sweater. I looked at Mam; at last, we had something in common! But the thought didn't make me happy.

"Well, now you know," she said, as if reading my thoughts correctly for once.

Oh, yes, I knew.

We sat together in my room, separated by similar thoughts about different men. When the phone rang, we both jumped.

Kev answered, talked rapidly and with unusual energy for a while, then called up, "Lyn? Anna - for you."

Relieved, I pulled on my dressing-gown, grabbed my glasses and ran down the stairs. As I picked up the phone, it all came back. Thursday, of course. How could I forget? Very easily when faced with a delinquent mother.

"Lyn - as you'll be home all day, you can monitor the media coverage for us." Typically Anna, she didn't wait to ask.

"Mmmm, all right. Local radio, regional TV, that sort of thing?"

"Yes. Keep a list - and notes - and switch stations around. Then get the local papers as soon as they're out this afternoon."

"They won't have the result in until tomorrow."

"They'll have coverage of the demo, though - perhaps photographs."

"Oh, yes . . . the demo," I said stupidly.

"You do remember? After all, it is about you."

"Is it?" I wasn't so sure. "Yeah, well . . . I'm only just getting myself together."

"Oh dear, bad mornings still?"

"Getting better. I saw Dr Ransome yesterday and passed all her tests."

"Oh, yes, Ma said you called in. Why didn't you wait?"

Why didn't I wait? Because I had such a soppy look on my face, that's why.

"I had to get back . . . you know . . ."

"Well, tell Kev I'll meet him at the side-gate, not the main drive. We have to be a bit surreptitious this time."

"Kev? What's he going to do?"

"Lyn, he's very useful. He has such a lot of political low cunning, learned from your mum, no doubt."

"But he's not a member of the SU, not even a student."

"So? We need all the support we can get."

"Yes, but isn't that secondary picketing or something?"

"O-oh, what's this? Naive little Lyn showing her political know-how?"

"I may not be an activist but nobody in our family can be politically naive. Even our Kev knows he shouldn't be there with you lot today."

"Well, I think that's his decision." She sounded just like our Mam.

"Yeah?" I wasn't convinced, but I didn't want to quarrel with a friend – my only friend. "Well, thanks for finding him the job, anyway."

"Rubbish, he'd have got it anyway."

"He'd probably never have heard of it. Networking's not exactly in his line."

She laughed, that low, gurgling laugh that always took me back to the shepherd's hut on the fell. "See you tonight, then."

"Tonight?"

"At home. Ma's laying on one of her great feasts – to celebrate or commiserate. Roger refuses to do either unless you're there. I think he feels you're sharing the same battle. Right, I must rush now. Keep up the good work!"

She was off.

So was Kev. He came rumbling down the stairs. "I'm off,

Mam," he called. "I'll be late tonight, we're celebrating at Anna's. See you there, Sis."

He slammed the door, then the gate, and was gone.

I peered upstairs to where Mam hovered at the top. I grinned at her. "Well, there's one of your problems solved, anyhow," I said.

Mam had her bath and got into her career-woman-outfit while I made some more coffee. We split yesterday's Guardian from the office and sat at the kitchen table reading and nibbling toast. For the first time in my life I felt close to her. Now and then we read bits of news out to each other but we didn't talk about Peter, or about Birkbeck. We just let it all alone. Like we always did.

"It'll never get better, if you pick at it," our Gran used to say when we fiddled with scratches and scabs. Perhaps that works for mental wounds too.

It was Gran herself who prevented further discussion. We heard her coming up the side of the house, puffing from the pull up the hill. As she opened the kitchen door, Mam stood up. "I'll be getting on then," she said and shot off upstairs.

"Was that your mam?" asked Gran. "She's going to be late."

"She had a few hours owing, so she had a lie-in."

"She sempt in a right rush to get away just now." Gran automatically started collecting pots from the table.

For the first time I wondered about Mam and Gran and Dad. There are more eternal triangles than the sexual one. Gran's always been an ever-present help in trouble to me, but she's been a pain to Kev; perhaps to Mam, too. Now she started bashing the pots about in the sink but even so I heard the ping of the phone and the murmur of Mam's voice out in the hall.

Then she popped her head round the kitchen door. "I'm off then, Lyn," she said. "'Bye now, Gran. I can't stop, I'm running late." She was flushed with rushing – or something.

Gran didn't look up. "I don't know why you're rushing now, Pam; you've already missed th' 'aff-past. There's only one every half-hour at this time in t'morning."

Mam looked startled. "Er . . . yes . . . I'll just have to walk down to the main road, then I can get any bus into the city. It'll be quicker than waiting."

She beamed at me. I knew she wouldn't have to walk far before Peter picked her up.

The plot thickens, I thought.

I was trying to concentrate on the two local stations on two radios when I caught the first report between boring disco pop and even more boring phone-ins.

"Reports are coming in of a student demo at Ripton College," said the DJ on Radio Halton. "More than three hundred students walked out of lectures this morning in support of Mr Robert Baxter, who faces a suspension hearing this afternoon. One of Mr Baxter's students, Rosalind Buggy, went missing from a field centre on the Peak. Rosalind was saved by the rescue services and is still too ill to continue her course at the college."

"He got your name wrong, lass," said Gran.

"And a lot else," I agreed. I wrote down all I could remember of the flash and turned my attention to the other radio, tuned into the local BBC. It was half an hour before they picked up the news, but at least they got the names right. I bent over my note-book, scribbling at a hell of a lick and thoroughly enjoying myself. There's something hypnotic about the clean white pages of a note-book and a newly sharpened pencil.

Gran got the lunch (tepid beans on cold toast) while I stayed with the media. The later reports merely repeated the earlier ones, until the one o'clock bulletin on Radio Halton.

"Members of the Board of Governors of Ripton College are having problems getting to the hearing at the college this afternoon. All entrances to the grounds have been blocked by demonstrating students. Mr Colin Cleaver, Chairman of the Enquiry, has just toured the picket lines, trying to persuade the students to return to lectures, but so far nobody has accepted the offer."

What was Anna thinking of? "She's having a lovely time playing power politics," Mam had said. I was beginning to think she was right. How far was Anna going? After all, if the hearing was abandoned today, neither Roger nor I would get back next week. The idea had its charms; I could think of some very pleasant ways of passing the time together. But as if she knew about my fantasies, Gran interrupted them.

"Eeh well, I'll go to the foot of our stairs," she exclaimed, pointing at the television.

I looked across the room and saw our Kev, walking with Anna at the head of a long line of students. They were shouting, waving banners, and heading towards the main entrance to college.

"Fancy your Kev, on telly," Gran looked quite proud of him, but then she frowned. "But why is he there? He's not at your college, is he? He might get wrong for trespassing or something..."

I rushed over and turned up the volume. We both watched, fascinated and appalled, as Kev led his troop up to the steps of the main entrance to college. Remembering what a fool I'd made of myself there, I could hardly bear to watch the media reporters making mince-meat of my brother. But he was just there to provide local colour for a confrontation between Anna and a local reporter.

"Mr Cleaver has accused the students of blocking the

process of democracy," she said. "What is your reaction to that?"

"Well, he would, wouldn't he?" Anna laughed at the quote. "Actually, the only people to have blocked democracy are the administrative officers of this college. Mr Cleaver himself ordered Lyn Bugge off the premises."

"Mr Cleaver tells us that the girl is off sick; she was back in hospital only yesterday, you know."

"Only as an out-patient. She's quite fit now, and trying to get on with her work ready for the exams later this month."

"So is this demonstration to support the girl's return to college or the lecturer's?"

Aahh – good point. I didn't know. Did Anna?

Anna tossed back a long strand of hair and looked straight into the camera.

"The demonstration is about democracy. It's about the fact that Lyn was suspended without a hearing, that Mr Baxter has been forced to neglect his students even though there's been no direct complaint against him. It's also about the fact that, time and time again, Mr Cleaver acts unilaterally. Mr Cleaver does not believe in student democracy, staff democracy, possibly not in any sort of democracy. We've never been given the opportunity for dialogue in this matter, or in any other. That's what we're demonstrating about."

So I was just a pawn in Anna's political campaign against Cleaver. 'Only interested in specimens,' Kev had warned. Right on there, old Kev; that's probably why she's interested in you: her sample of the unemployment problem in the industrial north. I suddenly felt a spurt of fury at the thought of Kev, bustling round like an enthusiastic pup, and Anna, coolly using him.

I was so deep into Kev's sufferings that I didn't even hear the phone ringing.

"It's that there feller wanting to talk to you," announced Gran, leaving the phone upturned on the stairs. "I'll keep conk for you in here, while you answer it." She settled herself with my note-book and glared at the TV screen.

"Hello?" I wondered who 'that there feller' would be. I daren't hope.

"Lyn? I'm just waiting for it all to begin. Needed a supportive word from my fellow-sufferer . . ."

"Oh, er . . . Roger." I said, supportively.

"Is that all?"

"No, er . . . you know I'll be thinking about you . . . hoping . . . oh, Roger, I'm that sorry." I was near to tears.

"Ach, Lyn, don't start that all over again. Nothing is your fault, remember that. Hey, I rang for your support and I end up handing it out to you!"

"I know, sorry." Oh, why was I such a wally when it came to words? I, who could scribble an act of a play in one evening, couldn't even find the right words to give comfort to a . . . friend.

"Don't be sorry about it," he said. "After all, it did bring us together, didn't it? It's an ill wind . . ."

"'Every cloud has a silver . . .'"

"There's more than one way to kill a pig . . . no, that's not right, is it?"

"It'll do, lad." I smiled into the telephone.

"And so will you, lassie. So long as you're thinking about me this afternoon, I'll be oll richt." His accent sounded thicker and his voice was husky, a bit uncertain.

So was I. "All right," I said, primly. "I s'll be thinking."

"So . . . 'bye Lyn . . . see you . . . tonight . . ."

"Ah . . .er . . . good luck. And I will be thinking . . . tha noahs."

"Aye, I'm verry certain of that."

The phone clicked; he was gone.

I sat on the bottom step, utterly relaxed. I was content now, to let the problems of our Kev, Anna, our Mam, even the inquiry drift past. Roger Baxter had telephoned me. Wow!

"You'll be well past your testing time, won't you, our Lyn?" Gran's voice cut through the romantic haze – or the low sugar level. I plodded upstairs for the gadgets. She was right; it was well past the testing time and the tests weren't marvellous either. I nipped downstairs for more insulin and caught the start of the next radio report.

"'Ark at that," said Gran. We heard the police sirens wailing, the raucous voices of the students chanting, and an irregular sharp clapping in the background. I thought of truncheons, and winced. "By guiney, it sounds as if it's got a bit out of hand," said Gran. "I hope our Kev's all right."

"Shhh . . ." I stood behind her, listening hard.

"The organised protest of this morning appears to have degenerated into mob violence," said an excited reporter. "Some students, apparently drunk, threw stones and broke windows. The police have now arrived and many students have drifted off. A firm core are sitting peacefully on the steps at the entrance to the college."

Was Anna sitting peacefully? Was Kev? Obviously the reporter wasn't going to tell us that. With the noise of riot in the background we were returned to the studio and an advert for Woolworths.

So much for secondary picketing. "Bloody fools!"

"Lyn! I won't have that."

"Sorry, Gran. But it sounds as if it's all backfired."

"You'll backfire if you don't get up them stairs and do your injection. Go on, I'll call you if anything happens."

But nothing did. During the afternoon there was a pile-up on the M1 and all reports were about that. The last we heard, before tea-time, was that the inquiry had begun, the demo had broken up and several students had been taken into custody.

Chapter 15

And we'd not had the local paper yet.

I left Gran in charge of the newsroom while I clattered down to the paper shop on my old bike. Kev's had gone with him that morning. Perhaps I could collect it from him while he was in prison? I rather fancied turning up at college on his super racer.

Always assuming I'd be allowed to turn up at college ever again, after Anna's great work today.

When I got back, the radios and TV were rumbling in the background while Gran rumbled in a deep sleep. I tiptoed through to the kitchen and put the kettle on. That woke her.

"Is that you, our Lyn?" she called. "There was nothink important on while you were out."

How could she know? Still an'all, I couldn't blame her; some cartoons were enough to make even the kids fall asleep.

"I'll bring some tea in and we'll check the papers next. OK, love?" I said.

They'd kept me an early edition at the shop. It didn't say much; just a short report about the planned demo and disruption of work. But the evening edition, out about four o'clock, carried headlines and photos on the front page.

We both read through the news as if preparing for an exam. She was searching for our Kev, and I was hunting for the result of the hearing. Neither of us found what we wanted; like life, really.

When the knocker on the front door clattered, we both jumped, as if it was our turn to be arrested.

I ran to the door, hoping it would be . . .

"Dad!"

"Hello, duck, I got a lift in." He crushed into the little hall and grinned at me. "Well, here's a turn up for the books, eh?"

I followed him into the front room. "I'm that surprised to see you," I said. That was the understatement of the year; for the first time in my life I wasn't delighted to see my dad.

"I bet you were more than surprised at the result of the hearing then. Hello, mother, orr raight?" He pottered off into the kitchen and sat down to take off his fell-boots.

"What d'you mean?" I asked. "It's not out yet, is it?"

"Aye, well, I heard it on a bulletin in t' Land Rover as we came in."

"So what is it?"

"You mean to say you 'aven't 'eard?"

"I wouldn't be asking if I had." It must have been on when I was at the paper shop and Gran was dozing.

"Well . . ." Dad pulled off his big wool sock and studied his foot as if reading his future. "Eeh, it's damned hard on your feet, this job, you know."

"Daaaad?"

"Yer what?" He grinned at me.

"No, don't tease, it's not funny!" I sounded quite hysterical even to myself.

"Nay, you're right there, lass," he agreed. "Come on into t' room and I'll tell you all about it."

Gran insisted on making more tea, and on making us wait for her until we discussed the news.

"Well, I suppose you could say he's won," announced Dad. "Cheers!" He tilted his mug in front of him and took a long drink of tea.

We both watched him put his mug down. "He did get his job back, d'y'see, but it seems there are conditions."

I felt a surge of relief flood through me. Conditions were nothing; I hadn't ruined Roger's career, that's what mattered. I heaved a great sigh. "Thank God for that," I said. I turned away from the light to hide my flushed cheeks and my foolish grin.

"What conditions?" asked Gran with a caution born of a lifetime's hard work and bad luck.

"Oh, I din't understand all them. I don't know how teachers are organised. Summat about doing an extra year, I gather . . . a repeated year, that's what it was. Do you know what that means, Lyn?"

I did. Anna had explained to me about the probationary year that teachers had to do before they finally qualified. She'd been pouring scorn on it because hardly anybody ever failed, even though plenty of our teachers were obviously incompetent.

"I think it means he won't actually be qualified until he's taught another year." Great, I thought. He'll be here at least another year. I hastily reorganised my Poly applications to include South Yorks, which I'd been determined to leave until now. I sat on the floor, at Dad's feet, in a haze of future plans for Roger and me . . . Fantasy time again!

"Is it, Lyn?" Dad's question brought me back.

"Is what?"

"Is it all Anna's fault that Kev's probably in prison right now?"

I thought about that. A month ago I'd have answered smartly that it was Kev's own decision, and therefore his own fault. I was always so certain about things then. But I knew, now, that it's not as simple as that. Look at our Mam. Look at me.

"Weeell," I said, "It all depends on what you mean by 'fault'."

Dad burst out laughing, just like he used to when I was a kid and came out with some 'old-fashioned' bit of wisdom. I hadn't heard him laugh that loud for a long time. For two years. "Eeh, our Lyn, if you could hear yourself. You used to be so full of your own opinions, allus ready to set the blame and to say so, loud and clear. A raight little big-gob you were. Now you're pussy-footing around like one of your mam's committees. You must be getting old, lass."

Before I could give him a typical gobfull, in memory of my youth, we heard footsteps and voices at the door. Alert, I also heard a car pulling away. I glanced at Dad, still ruddy and beaming from his joke. And I wanted to freeze that moment like you do on the video. If only nothing else followed, I thought, we'd all be all right now.

"This must be your mam," he said, happily.

It was. And it was our Kev. How do they do it? I thought. Always managing to meet up and come home together. And in whose car?

"Hello, love," Dad said.

She froze; it could have been with surprise, it could have been with shock. "What on earth are you doing here?" she asked. It wasn't an unusual greeting from our Mam; she always likes things to be orderly; she hates surprises, even nice ones.

"I got a lift in," he said. "I thought I'd best be home

tonight, to hear all the goings-on. Mind, I didn't think there'd be this many." He looked over at Kev, who was on his way from the kitchen, unzipping his soaked anorak. He must have been round the back with his bike.

I looked around the room: Dad, still beaming, giving off that calm hugeness that outdoor people always seem to have about them, Mam, neatly tucked into the other armchair, pale and tense, her eyes looking nowhere, seeing nothing.

"D'you want a cup of tea, Pam?" asked Gran. Mam shook her head, wearily. Gran started clearing the mugs. I was sure she'd sense something in the air. "And what about you, our Kev?" she added.

"What about me?" he asked. "Did you see me on telly?"

"We did that," she said grimly. She pushed past him into the kitchen. Kev looked at me and winked. I stared stonily back.

"So you didn't end up in jail, after all?" I said.

"Nah, it was just the usual drunken lot who got carted off. The rest of us – the peaceful protesters – were just left alone. We sat it out until the result, even though it was siling down. That's why I need a bath, even me underpants is soaked." He laughed and looked all round at us. "I s'll have to have the first bath, our Lyn. You can follow on. I'll mek sure I leave you some hot water."

"Where's you two off then?" asked Dad.

"To Anna's party – celebration – it'll be a right to-do."

"A right to-do!" said Gran, pottering in with her coat on. She always decided when to leave; usually, I now realised, soon after Mam came in. "I'd say there's been enough to-dooment in this family lately to last a whole year." There was a warning tone in her voice. I wondered how much she knew.

"I'll just go down with me mother," Dad said quietly. Somebody always took Gran home, to settle her in for the

143

night, though I could never think why. Any burglar coming face to face with our Gran would find himself faced with a lecture on Marxism today and two slapped wrists. "Then I'll bring some fish and chips. Save you cooking," he added without looking at Mam.

"Then you two can have an evening in peace while we live it up," said Kev. He rushed off upstairs, singing 'We shall overcome' like an old campaigner.

As soon as they left, I thought about ringing Roger. I knew I'd be seeing him at the party very soon but I wanted to talk to him on his own first. But what if Roger didn't want to speak to me on my own? I pondered the problem.

While I was dithering, Mam beat me to it. As if an electric current had been run through her, she shot up and off to the phone. She was still talking urgent and low when Kev called me up to the bathroom. I crept past her on the stairs, feeling, without really looking, the glow on her face. Well, I knew what caused that, well enough.

After a shower – Kev had used all the hot water, of course – I scrabbled through my wardrobe – a quick enough job in my case. For once I cursed my lack of interest in clothes; I must have been the only pupil at school who actually liked uniform. At college, I invented my own uniform and stuck with it: jeans, Kev's cast-off shirts, my Arran or a sweatshirt, trainers or boots. My beautiful ski-jacket was the jewel; it was crinkly silk, emerald and navy. Wearing that, I didn't care about what was underneath. But I couldn't wear it to a party.

Mam would have a shirt, or a sweater, I knew. I listened, not meaning to overhear, just checking whether I could ask her to lend me her best silk shirt. I put my head round my door and peered downstairs. She was still sitting there, the phone now beside her. I could hear her quietly weeping.

Oh hell! What should I do?

I decided to go ahead. One posh shirt against my mother's tears. "Maam? Can you lend me anything so's I can look decent at this do?"

I heard her sniff, blow her nose hard, and start upstairs.

"You're in for a cold, Mam," Kev called from his room at the end of the landing. Our house is that small you can't even weep in private. I grinned at her, sympathetically.

"Come on in here, let's see what I've got." She led the way into their bedroom. The big bedroom we called it, though by the time it had a wardrobe, two chests and a double bed, there was no room left over. Mam riffled through the hangers in the wardrobe. "Wearing jeans, I suppose?" she said brightly, like a shop assistant. I noticed she'd shut the door.

"Lyn, try to make sure that you and Kev aren't back before midnight, will you?" She spoke softly.

At any other time it would have been funny. I mean, going off to a party and being asked to stay out late!

"I'll try, but we might not come home together," I pointed out. "Kev won't want to be with me all evening . . ." and I certainly didn't want him hanging round Roger and me.

"I'll pay for a taxi for you both," she offered. "You don't have to spend the whole evening together, just arrange to meet up when you want to come home. Please, Lyn, we need some time to talk, your Dad and me."

I looked at her face, reflected in the mirror. Winter never suited her sallow complexion; now, she looked what Gran would have called 'sought-into', with hollow cheeks and shadows under her eyes.

"What . . .?" But I didn't want to hear her plans just then. "What shall I wear?" I amended the question hastily.

"The red silk shirt'll look good with your decent jeans,"

she said, loudly, "and you can take my navy mohair in case it's cold."

"Right," I agreed. "Shan't be long now, Kev!"

I was quite amazed when I looked into the long mirror in the big bedroom and saw myself in scarlet. Luckily I did possess a pair of soft leather patchwork pumps, supposedly slippers, but decent enough for a party.

Although it was winter, it was wet and muggy, so I decided to go without socks or coat. Mam lent us her umbrella to get to the bus and gave Kev instructions for us to come home by taxi.

"Oh, hell, Mam, we might not want to come home at the same time," he protested.

"Then one of you will have to walk," she said, smiling. "There's only enough money for one taxi."

"Are you all set, Lyn?" he asked. "You've done all your things?"

I tossed my newly-washed head and didn't answer. Of course I'd done all the testing and injecting before we left. And for once I'd remembered to pack supplies in the navy leather bag Mam had lent me.

"'Bye then, Mam," called Kev, from the hall. "I'll see she gets home all right."

"'Bye, Lyn." Mam gave me a long look. "Have a good time. It's grand to see you going out at last. It'll do you good. Give my congratulations to Roger and to Anna."

She reached up and brushed some bits off my shoulders. "Er . . . thanks . . . for listening. It helped, you know . . . to get things straight."

She finished brushing me down and stood smiling sadly. I thought she was about to kiss me, but she didn't. Not Mam.

Chapter 16

There was no mistaking the house this time. Cars were parked solidly up the street, and the steady beat of music filtered down the drive. The curtains were still un-drawn and every window blazed. Even at a glance, each room seemed crammed with people, whose voices made a shrill background to the music.

I suddenly felt quite sick; this was not my scene; never had been. I couldn't stand loud music even when Grandad took me to the Brass Band Festival up in Barnsley; I disgraced him then, by sitting with my fingers in my ears and leaving a puddle on the floor. At that moment I felt I might just do it again.

"It's all right, Sis," Kev said. "They're a good crowd, honest." And he took my hand and squeezed it.

"Hi – come in!" A tall, stringy man stood at the door with a long stick of bread in his hand. "Drinks in the kitchen, food in the dining-room on your right. Coats etc upstairs. I'm Adrian – and you?"

"I'm Kevin Bugge – this is my sister, Lyn." Kev managed

that quite nicely, I thought. I reckoned without the effect on Adrian.

"Wow! Hey everybody, she's here!" Adrian called right down the hall.

The music stopped; heads peered out of the rooms either side of the hall, from the kitchen, even from upstairs. It was like a nightmare; I glanced down, half expecting to be naked.

"Go on." Kev gave me a push into the narrow hall. What then? Was I supposed to walk the length of it, nodding graciously side to side? Should I sign autographs? I felt sweat breaking out on my neck and worried about the collar of Mam's best shirt.

"Lyn . . . Lyn . . ." Anna pushed easily through the crowd. I wish I was tall and dominating! "Oh, it's good to see you at last." She pulled me towards her and gave me a great hug, just there, in public. I smiled as much as I could and vaguely patted the middle of her back, as if she had wind. "Look everybody," she cried, "the girl of the moment!"

Then they all cheered and people's hands were held out to me, as Anna hugged my shoulders and led me along the hall. I could feel Kev following on; I could also feel his disappointment that Anna hadn't even noticed him yet. As if I hadn't enough to worry about.

We made it at last to the kitchen and Anna thrust a glass of something in my hand. It was removed before I could even take a sip.

"Steady on, have you allowed for wine in today's intake?"

The voice made me shiver; his touch, as he leaned over my shoulder and took the glass, burnt my hand.

"Roger," I whispered.

"And this is Kev – your brother?" he asked chattily,

avoiding my eyes. Why, what had I done now? He turned away. "Hi, Kev. Perhaps you'd like the wine?"

"Is there any beer?" asked Kev.

"Sure. There's even a keg of Old Peculiar. Anna, show a bit of sense and get the lady a Diet Coke while I draw Kev a pint."

"Oh, Lord, sorry, Lyn. I was carried away for a moment. Cheers!" Anna reached over to the long table, which was covered in bottles, and poured my coke.

"Cheers!" I said, and drank the whole glass off fast.

"I say, is thirst a side-effect of the diabetes, or the treatment?" she asked with professional interest.

"Stress, I think. Your hall seemed like a mile long just then."

"Oh, Lyn, you'll never make a social butterfly, will you?" She smiled down at me. A strand of her ashen hair fell forward and she flipped it back in the sort of gesture I'd always dreamed of making . . . "Well, come on and meet a few people."

I didn't want to meet a few people; I wanted to wait for Roger to return, but I could see nothing but chests and boobs from my level. And none belonged to him.

Anna led me around the other rooms, introducing me to various Boffs whose names I heard but was too flummoxed to remember. The party obviously continued upstairs because Anna was called up there and she left me in the dining-room facing a laden table and a large man with grey-flecked black hair.

"Bugge, eh? You must be Pamela Bugge's daughter?" he said, looking me up and down. I wondered if he recognised the shirt.

"Yes, I am." My one claim to fame.

"Aye, she's a grand lass, your mam. You must be proud of her."

Must I? Was I? Embarrassed, perhaps; irritated, often; but proud? Never.

"I'm Ron Whittle, Area Health." He was old-fashioned enough to hold out his hand. I wiped my sweaty palm on the back of my jeans and shook hands.

"Yes," he went on. "Your mam's a force to be reckoned with on the Health Committee."

"She's a force to be reckoned with at home," I answered, a bit grim.

He laughed. Had I made a joke? I stared at him, amazed he should find me so entertaining.

"I'll bet she is an'all," he said. "I've had my clashes with her on and off, and I can't think of anybody I'd rather clash with. Lovely lady, she is."

He didn't exactly wink; he didn't nudge nudge; he didn't need to. I knew what he was thinking – and about my mam! I blushed for her – was it for her?

"I s'll miss her when she goes off to university."

I looked round quickly, but Kev must be sticking near the beer, thank goodness. What if he heard? How many more people at that party knew about Mam?

"You did know about her award?" He was looking at me very closely.

"Oh, yes, I knew," I said. "It's just that she ... er ... she doesn't want it broadcast, you know. She's a bit shy."

His black eyes shone with disbelief. Pam Bugge, scourge of the rate-capped council, shy?

". . . about the award," I said. "About getting a university place, when there's so many cuts," I said, inventing motives as if she was a character in one of my stories.

"Aye, I can understand that. She's got principles, has your mam."

Oh, yes, we all knew about Mam's principles. Why, at

this very moment she would be arguing about them to poor Dad.

"I think I'll just have a bit to eat. I have to keep my sugar-levels up," I said. Well, that's the first time I've used the old condition as an excuse. I must have been desperate.

"Aye, it's very wise to keep eating; mops up the alcohol, you know."

He looked as though he was ready to mop up some more alcohol. "Shall I fetch you a drink?" he asked.

"No, I'll just eat for the moment."

I watched as he edged out of the room. I tried to calculate the odds on him bumping into Kev, recognising him, talking about Mam, and letting the news out. A hundred to one? Gran would be able to work that out, I couldn't.

I took a hunk of garlic bread and chewed on it. Nobody else seemed to be interested in the food. They were all talking at each other. I took a stick of celery and moved off. I didn't want to spend the rest of the evening hearing all about my wonderful mother from Ron.

I peered into the room with the music. It was very dark and empty of furniture. It was full of bodies though, some turning and twisting alone, others shrugging a shoulder, standing close, moving smoothly together. Something else I couldn't do.

"Shall we dance, tra-la-la?"

My stomach churned, my spine crumbled, I caught my breath.

"I can't," I said flatly to Roger.

"Yes you can," he said. "Everybody can dance; you just do what you like, jump about, twirl around, or jog on the spot. What's your choice?"

We stood opposite each other sort of jogging slightly. I felt the beat of the music right through the floor-boards, and without looking at him, I did a few variations on my footwork.

"There you are, you're better at it than I am." He reached out and held my shoulders. I was ready for him to pull me close, but he kept his arms stiff, almost pushing me away from him. I concentrated on the middle button of his shirt and gritted my teeth. All over, I thought; he's got his job back, Anna's made her political stand, I'm back on my own, like I was on the field course.

The music rose up to a hysterical shriek as I gyrated away from Roger, to dance on my own. But he followed my lead into the darkest corner of the room. "Lyn." I saw him mouth my name but I couldn't hear until he bent over and spoke into my ear; not, however, sweet nothings. "There's a lot I want to say to you, but perhaps we ought to be a bit tactful – college gossip – you know?"

"I don't care about that." I lifted my head up and looked right into his face, bent over me. In the dusky lighting his face glowed white, his eyes nearly disappeared in their deep sockets, his silky black hair fell onto his face. I wanted to melt into the waxed floorboards at that moment.

"Well, I care about you, Lyn. I've caused you enough trouble this term." Taking my hand, he led me to the middle of the floor where the music was loudest. I saw his mouth move again. "Later," he said, looking straight at me and widening his eyes. I nodded.

"Go it, Lynnie!" That must be Gary Baldwin; nobody else used that name. "'S better than climbing hills with him, in't it?"

Roger grinned at me and steered me to the door. "Food," he announced. "Then we'll find a quiet place to talk." He slung my cardigan round me and left his arm on my shoulders. So much for college gossip, I thought.

There was a queue by now, in the dining room, and as we moved slowly up to the food, Roger was kept busy talking to other people, who edged their way past us carrying paper plates full of salads and bread. I was so busy planning what I was going to eat that I didn't talk. Before we reached the table, however, a small, bearded man stopped to talk. He nodded to me as if he knew me, but he spoke only to Roger.

"Well, now you're free, it'll be good to have you on the team, Roger," he said. "We need a geologist up there, and you'll find the climbing quite a challenge even for you."

Then I remembered where I had seen him. He had driven the Land Rover the day we'd gone up to the fells. On the way home they'd discussed some expedition and he'd offered Roger a place when he lost his job. But Roger hadn't lost his job.

"Roger... Roger... you're needed for the beer... a new keg." Anna's voice rose over the buzz of conversation.

"Sorry, Lyn, you must get something to eat. I'll be back . . ." With a squeeze of my shoulder, Roger left.

I moved up the queue, puzzling over the bit of conversation I'd heard. Where was 'up there'? And who needed a geologist? Why was Roger going to be free? He'd got his job back, hadn't he? I suddenly lost interest in the food. I left the queue and went off to find a quiet place to think.

There was only the front porch. Although it was a wet winter night, it was very mild. I pulled Mam's best mohair back round me and perched on the doorstep. I was suddenly very thirsty, but I couldn't face the battle to the kitchen for another Coke. Or was it that I couldn't face Roger?

I took off my smeared glasses and cleaned them with Mam's hankie. There was something happening that I wasn't in on; something that wasn't being said. I might lack a certain sophistication – an *enfant sauvage*, as Anna called me; but I have enough experience to know when I'm left out of things. But what was I left out of this time? And why? And did I really want to know?

"There's things you're better off not knowing, our Lyn,"

Gran always said when she thought I was asking too many personal questions. "Ignorance is . . ."

"'Allo, 'allo. Vye is zees young laidy 'ere all alone?" Gary Baldwin peered at me from the front door.

"She's having a quiet sit down, Monsieur Baldwin, so bog off!"

Gary laughed too much; he looked like he'd been at the Old Peculiar. "I thought you'd be snogging away in some quiet room upstairs with Sir," he leered, with that uncanny nose for the truth that drunks sometimes have. "Budge up, then." He pushed his bum alongside me on the step.

"Don't be daft," I said. "And they say women gossip! You'd beat Mother Tuckett any old day." Mrs Tuckett used to spy on us when we were kids, and tell on us too. "You want to watch that wagging tongue of yours, it'll get you into trouble one of these days."

"That depends where I wag it, Lynnie Bugge. I wouldn't half mind it wagging a bit in your direction." He leaned heavily on me and breathed beer fumes.

"Oh, gerroff, Gary. You never fancied me in your life."

"Praps not before, but you're different now. You're famous."

I looked at him, amazed, then fell to laughing long and loud. I'd read about sexual politics but one mention in the local paper didn't turn Lynnie Bugge into Jackie Collins.

"Nay, give over laughing," protested Gary. "You must have more sex-appeal than you ever let on to us. Look at what you've made Sir do."

I felt cold all over. What could he mean? Surely nobody, not even my family, not even nosey-parker Gary could have sussed out our relationship? Come to that, I wasn't even sure we had a relationship. "So what have I made Sir do, according to your twisted little mind?"

"Oh . . tha knaws . . ." Gary made a vague gesture upwards.

"No, Gary, I don't know. I've not been in college for weeks, you know." That was quite good, I thought. Gary would assume I had no connection with Sir now.

"So he didn't do it for you, then? Oh . . . must have been on account of Boffy Anna."

"What did he do?" I grated the words out slowly, though I was shaking with impatience.

"Do? Well, that's what all this is for, in't it?" This time Gary flung out both arms as if to embrace the whole party. "To celebrate him putting one on old Cleaver." He fell heavily against me, and I pushed him back against the door post.

"How did he do that, Gary?" I asked, looking at him closely.

"Well, by resigning, of course. After they give 'im 'is job back, he told them where to shove it. Eehh, I'd like to 'ave been a fly on Old Cleaver's wall when he told 'em." He giggled and hiccupped into my hair.

I sat quite still. That was what no one was telling me. Roger had got his job back, but he wasn't taking it. He was going off on that expedition. That's what the chap in the queue was talking about. That's what everybody at the party, everybody in college knew, except me. Roger Baxter was leaving town, trailing clouds of snook-cocking glory, throwing away a career I'd worried myself sick over. I needn't have bothered.

"Come on." I pulled Gary to his feet. He was one of the few people who don't tower over me. "Let's dance."

So we did. We danced the wild gyrations, the jogging on the spot, even the smooching in the corner. And between dancing, Gary topped up his beer, and fed me with sticky concoctions based on Coke. I hoped it was diet Coke, and drank freely. After Gary belched into my ear and rushed off upstairs, I realised I couldn't stay still, or perhaps the room was wobbling? I was sweating buckets, even though I had long ago lost Mam's mohair. At the thought of Mam, I decided it was time to get home. I had to find Kev and a taxi and we'd get home and everything would be all right.

I staggered out of the dance room, into the hall. It seemed very long again, as it had at the beginning of the party, but I held on to the wall and slithered towards the kitchen.

"Lyn – here you are, I've been looking for you everywhere. What's this I hear about Mam?" Kev's reddened face was pushed into mine, his beery breath made me flinch.

"I...I..." I reached out to him and threw up all over his shirt. I remember hoping I'd missed Mam's silk one, and then very little else.

Chapter 17

Of course they all thought I was pissed.

That's the trouble with a hypo: you appear to be drunk. You have all the symptoms: loss of balance, blurred speech, irrational reactions, and, of course, the spewing up. Kev backed away from me, brushing unmentionable slops off his shirt.

"Bloody hell, Lyn, what d'you think you're doing? You've been drinking."

I tried to defend myself, but the pins and needles around my mouth prevented me. I shook my head and dreamily watched blue lights flash around Kev's shoulders.

"Lyn... Lyn..." I could hear Kev shouting to me but it didn't seem to matter.

Until he grabbed hold of me. Then it mattered so much that I shoved him off and made for the door. When he tried to stop me, I felt a surge of fury and kicked out hard, noting with passing interest that I was barefoot.

"That feller bothering you, duck?" asked a passing lad. If my lips could have moved I'd have laughed. Bother? Oh, no bother. Just my brother in a paddy and me in a hypo; nothing we can't handle.

Eventually, Kev held on long enough to get me to the stairs. Faces peered up as we fought our way from step to step. They were enjoying the entertainment, but I saw only glimpses of evil grins through the bars of the balustrade.

Kev pulled me up to the landing. My head lolled on his chest, my lips wouldn't move, my eyelids were too heavy to lift. "Your bag, Lyn, where's your bag?" He kept yelling and shaking me.

Julia Hitchens took over. She led us into a bedroom, out of everybody's way. "Here, drink this," she ordered me.

I took the glass of golden fizz and glogged the lot. "Nice . . ." I beamed up at her. "Nighty night." And I fell back on the bed. All I wanted to do was to be left alone to sleep. She leaned over me. For a moment I thought she was going to tuck me in and kiss me, like Gran used to when I was a little girl. Instead she slipped her arm round my back and hauled me to my feet. She might look as if the next breeze would carry her off, but she was tough.

"Come on, Lyn," she said. "You must stay awake now until we find your insulin." She turned to Kev. "My guess would be the kitchen. Everybody went there first for drinks and there were a few bags lying about."

"I'll go and get it. Keep her going," he ordered.

She started off round the bedroom with me. "We have to walk a bit, Lyn," she said gently. So I did. I'd have done anything for her. She poured me another lovely drink and I felt a bit better.

Anna came in, looking fraught. "Oh Ma, there's been some thieving. How could they? People you think you know, people you trust? How could they?"

"Lyn's bag?" Julia asked quietly.

"And several others. Adrian says there were quite a few

near the fridge earlier on. They've all gone now." She sounded near to tears. I peered round, trying to see the effect, but the room spun and I clutched hold of Julia.

"Whooops! Perhaps some kind person put them away?" she suggested, catching me as I swayed.

"And perhaps some rotten sod pinched them. Ma, we've looked everywhere in the house. What shall we do?"

"We'd better get her home as soon as we can. She must have insulin there."

"Bound to. You gave her the Lucozade? I'll find some sweets; somebody told me Mars Bars are best. She'll be all right." Anna dismissed me and my boring condition. "It's the thieving that's worrying me."

Stung by Anna's dismissal or revived by the Lucozade, I suddenly straightened up. "I'm quite all right. Just leave me alone and I'll be fine!" I shouted, flinging Julia's helping arm off my shoulder.

There was an embarrassed pause and Anna murmured something about "normal reaction" to her mother. "Come on, then, if you're all right," she said. "Get yourself downstairs and I'll run you home."

"No . . . taxi . . . got to get a taxi . . ."

"What on earth for?"

I swayed against a wardrobe, thinking about that one. I knew we had to get a taxi . . . after midnight . . . but I couldn't think why.

"What time is it?" I asked.

"Half eleven. Why?"

"Can't go yet. Midnight. Taxi."

"You mean you've got one booked for then?" Julia asked.

I shook my head, but gently.

Anna's attention was now focussed on crime. "For goodness sake, Lyn, you have to get home. Your bag's gone missing and with it your insulin."

And with it our taxi-fare, I thought, with a rare flash of intelligence. "Home then, James," I gesticulated wildly. "And don't spare the..."

I crashed down on the bed again. Wave after wave of nausea hit me, cold sweat oozed into the silk shirt, the bed tipped and turned as if it was a raft on a very rough river. From a distance I heard Kev's gruff voice. Kev always sounds as if he's angry, even when he's not. Tonight he was.

"What sort of friends have you got?" he shouted at Anna. "Nob'dy up at Norton 'd pinch handbags at a party. A right load o' riff-raff these folk are."

"Oh... do shut up, Kevin. There are more important things at issue than the old chestnut of class distinction."

"Aye, there's Mam's best leather handbag at issue, and our Sis's life-support. But they won't be big enough issues for you to tek on, will they?"

"Don't you patronise me, you stupid little chauvinistic..."

When she slammed the door, it sounded like the clanging of a bank vault in my ears.

Isn't it lovely how, in moments of need, your family and best friends rally round? I tried to shift my numb facial muscles into a grin. I knew our Kev'd never make it with Anna. I even felt sorry for the bloke who did.

Julia's fine-boned face floated across in front of me. She handed me a biscuit. "Eat this, now, and you'll feel better."

"No! Nothing to eat," I said. I squashed the biscuit up and scattered the crumbs all over the bed. "Lessgo, Kev!"

"I'm ever so sorry for all this, Mrs Hitchens," said Kev. "She doesn't mean it, you know."

Creep! I thought. Why don't they all go away and let me sleep?

"I'd lend you my car," Julia said. "But you mustn't drive if you've had more than a couple of beers."

"It wouldn't make any difference," he answered. "I can't drive."

I winced for him. Every time he got on a new work scheme, Kev planned to take his driving test. Usually before the third lesson, he was out of work again. The jobs never lasted; Kev's burning desire to drive always did.

"So Lyn's idea of a taxi seems to be the best." She smiled down at me. I was counting and breathing, like they taught me in hospital. If you breathe deeply and slowly, you relax and any sugars left in the bloodstream can work more effectively. It was all calming down a bit now; the bed was floating slightly and my heart was thudding, but I knew I could cope.

"Taxi, Kev, get a taxi. Mam said . . ." I shouldn't have mentioned that name. Not to Kev. Not just then.

Poor Kev, standing there in somebody's old tee-shirt, his corkscrew curls shaking around his blazing blue eyes. "Aye, and that an'all," he shouted at me. "There's things our Mam's said I know nowt about. D'you?"

I sighed, trying to summon up the energy to tackle this most important moment. Was it always going to be like this, I wondered? Was I going to be in a diabetic hypo at every important moment of my life?

There was no answer to that. Only the flurry of footsteps on the stairs and the door flung open as Roger Baxter strode in, rolled me in the blanket, and picked me up like a parcel.

"Come on, Kev. I've got the Mini out – OK, J.? Lyn'll be home and dosed up in twenty minutes."

And we set off downstairs, just like that!

I closed my eyes. Well, what else could I do? Fight and scream as if I was being abducted? And if I was, by him, would I care? I felt there was somehing I could have protested about, to Roger Baxter, something to make me angry . . . I gave up trying to think. I lay in his arms, wrapped like a child, in a warm blue blanket. I hoped there were a lot of stairs to go down.

"Here, chew on this," said Anna as she met us in the hall. She shoved a mini-Mars Bar into my hand. "I'll ring tomorrow about the bag . . . and things. Oh Lyn, I am sorry." She was, too. Tears stood on the rims of her clear grey eyes. I vaguely patted her arm and shook my head. There was a lot I wanted to say to her, but I couldn't summon up the energy.

Now, snuggled in the blanket, sucking the chocolate and watching Roger's hands on the wheel, I felt quite content.

I should have known it wouldn't last.

Chapter 18

As soon as Roger pulled in by our gate, Kev shot out of the car and up the path. He was off to tackle our Mam, now that he thought he'd solved all my problems.

Not that he has, I thought, pushing his seat forward. I reached for the catch to open the door. Lucozade and the Mars Bar had helped but I was still sweating with every move.

"Wait!" Roger stayed my hand. "I need to talk to you, Lyn."

I shook my head wearily. "As soon as our Kev tells them I was drunk Dad'll be out here."

"Ted? Isn't he up on the Peak?"

"He came home to hear the news – your news."

"Our news."

"Is it?"

"Well of course it is; it concerns us both, doesn't it?"

I remembered why I should feel angry at Roger Baxter.

"You're not coming back, are you?" I said.

"Ah, you've heard."

"Not from you I haven't."

"Lyn, I wanted to tell you myself. I'd hoped to be with you at the party, you know, alone. I wanted . . . ach, Lyn . . ." We sat in silence for a moment, then he sighed.

In the glare of the street light I saw him leaning on the steering wheel, resting his head on his hand. Dad used to sit like that for hours at the kitchen table, pretending to look for jobs in the paper, but really looking at nothing.

I heard the click of our front door opening.

"Dad's coming now," I said.

He gave a deep shuddering sigh. "Lyn, tomorrow – can you come out walking? Will you be well enough?"

"Is there any point?"

"You know there is. Look, I'm sorry about tonight, about my bad timing . . ." The gate clicked and Dad approached. "Ten o'clock – I'll beg the car and pick you up." Roger turned to face me. "And Lyn, I do have plans and I'd like them to concern you, too." He leaned over and squeezed my shoulder, then opened the passenger door.

"Hello, Ted. We can't go on meeting like this, can we?" he greeted Dad as he got out.

"Either that or we'll have to study medicine," Dad laughed.

I was that relieved to hear him laugh. Then anxious again. Why was he laughing, after what Mam must have told him? Was it a bitter laugh? I tried to remember it.

"Coom on, now, lass, let's be 'aving you." He reached in and eased me out of the Mini.

Standing on the pavement, clutching the blue blanket around me, I leaned against him. My dad. I felt suddenly choked. "Ohhhh, Daad," I wailed softly, so's not to waken the neighbours. "Somebody's pinched Mam's bag and all my equipment. All that stuff you paid for . . ."

"Nay, nay, lass. Don't fratch. It's probably nobbut lost."

I hitched my blanket up and shuffled to the gate. One quick look back and a little finger-waggle to Roger. What an exit!

"I'll sort out the handbag mystery," he called, loud enough to waken several neighbours. "It's just the usual dossing about, you know. I'll be carrying it back to you tomorrow, nae doubt."

"See you tomorrow . . . and tomorrow . . . and tomorrow . . ." I thought, hazily and inaccurately.

"Well, what have you been up to, our Lyn?" asked Mam when I got in. I could have asked her the same question. There was something cat-like about the way she was draped in her soft velour dressing-gown, peering up at me through her damp, black fringe. She must have just had a bath, I thought.

"Nay, let her get herself sorted out," Dad said, firmly.

To my surprise she did.

In the kitchen Kev was making tea and buttering teacakes. My old supplies of testers, syringes and strips were already out on the draining board.

"As soon as I've finished," said Kev, "you can do your injection in here then come and have a bit of supper."

"Thanks." I moved across to the sink. "And . . . Kev . . . I'm sorry I made such a mess of your shirt – and your party." I was whispering now. "Was I really drunk, Kev? Or was it the diabetes?"

"That and the stuff that idiot Gary was filling you up with. You wait till I see him!"

But the threat wasn't serious; Kev whistled under his breath as he worked; he looked more relaxed than he had all evening. Why? What had he said to Mam? More important, what had she said to him? And to Dad?

It was like waiting for the next episode of a soap. But it would have to wait until all my routine was complete. Kev mashed the tea, loaded up his tray and winked at me as he went off to the front room.

I nipped across the back lobby to the outside lavatory. Urine test – high, but not as high as I thought it would have been. Back in the kitchen, thumb-prick, blood test; still lower than expected. Well done, Lucozade; that'll be my party tipple from now on. I tore open a new syringe and inserted it into the bottle of milky insulin. Trust Kev to know the long-lasting stuff. I let the blanket drop, pulled down my jeans, squeezed a nice bit of thigh and plunged the needle in. Wow! I'd forgotten, even in one week, the sting of that prick. My new gadgets were so smooth and simple.

I felt a sudden spurt of anger as I remembered what I'd lost: not only Mam's best handbag (and, come to that, where was her best mohair?), not only my emergency insulin, but hundreds of pounds-worth of technology, paid for with Dad's redundancy money. The thought of some ignorant thieving sod pocketing my taxi-fare and ditching my valuable injector-pen made me seeth. If I find out who did it, I promised myself, I shall personally bash him, be he ever so tall!

Thus fortified with insulin and thoughts of revenge I zipped up my jeans, threw all the bits into the bin, slung Julia Hitchens' blanket toga-wise around me and entered the arena of our front room.

I could have cut the drama. There they were sitting cosily by the fire eating teacake and supping tea!

"'Ere she is, looking better already," said Dad.

"Well, sit yourself down by me and have a bit of supper. Mek you feel better in the morning," said Kev.

"You sound just like our gran," I told him as I sat down on the settee.

Mam said nothing. I looked quickly across at her, trying to gauge her mood. But her hair fell across her face as she bent to drink her tea. She finished drinking and stretched back in her chair with a long – was it languorous? – sigh.

I looked from her to Dad. He munched a buttered tea-cake and smiled to himself. I couldn't make it out. All night I'd been thinking about them 'facing up to things', worrying about Dad slipping back into depression, and here they were cosy as an advert for cocoa. I drank my tea, thoughtfully.

"Have a tea-cake with that, our Lyn; you need it." Even Kev sounded gentle.

I took the tea-cake he offered me and looked questioningly at him.

"Did you know all about Mam?" he asked.

Oh, yes. I knew all about Mam. But did he? Did they?

I shot a look across to the lady herself.

"Oh yes, Lyn knows. I told her first when we were getting her ready for the party. Didn't I, Lyn?"

I could only nod. She didn't tell them why she'd had to tell me. She hadn't mentioned Peter.

"Of course," she went prattling on, "I'd planned to discuss it with all of you at the weekend, but what with Dad coming home so sudden . . ."

Her voice softened and she looked straight across at Dad. She smiled, she glowed, she . . . well, she sort of flirted. I looked at her more closely, at her high colour, her bright eyes; were they the result of her bath? Or the fire? Or had they . . .?

I caught my breath. I was sure that's what they had been doing. 'Facing up to things' indeed. The more I thought about it, the surer I became. Hence Dad's happy laugh, Mam's bath, her relaxed air.

"Well, what have you got to say?" Kev nudged me hard.

"What? To say?" I asked stupidly.

"Eeh, I'd have thought with all your women's lib stuff,

you'd be over the moon about Mam going off to university, even before you do."

"Ooh . . . that . . . well, yes, of course I am."

"You don't sound it."

"Oh, yes, I am. But it's not news to me, is it? I've done all the congrats before."

"Yes, she has done all the congrats, Kev, so stop nagging like an old mother hen," Mam said. "I know our Lyn's pleased to see me striking out on my own, aren't you, love?"

For once I got the hidden message. So . . . Peter was out of the running. I felt a pang of sympathy for him, remembering how I'd felt when I heard that Roger was striking out on his own.

"I am glad – for both of you," I answered, looking right at her. Clever stuff this code, I thought.

"Well, there'll be some changes round here, with Mam away at the college, Dad away on his course and me working. What's our Lyn going to do?" Kev looked round, just like he used to when he was a lad, when we were planning an outing or a holiday and we couldn't all agree. Kev hated anybody to be left out.

"She's going to get her A-levels, aren't you, luv?" Dad said.

"Not unless I get a hell of a lot more work done in the next term," I admitted.

"Yeah, but then?" Kev looked sharply at me. He'd seen Roger with me tonight; perhaps he knew a bit more than he was letting on.

He didn't know about Mam and Peter though. Well, if she had diplomatic immunity, so had I. I'd say nowt.

"Lyn can't decide that just now. She's got exams to go through and grades to get. You never know with A-Levels; best to keep your options open for the next six months. Eh, Lyn?" Mam raised her beautifully-shaped eyebrows at me.

Was that a signal? If it was, I couldn't interpret it. I was already out of my depth.

"Er... I might decide to take a year out after A-levels," I said casually. It was a good time to lay a few foundations. "I've not decided about the Poly yet."

I waited for Mam's scathing comments about my dithering as usual, but she just smiled a wise sort of smile and nodded in agreement. So I smiled back and suddenly felt the surge of warm pride I used to feel for Mam when I was a kid. I hadn't felt like that about her since... a long time.

"Eeh, it's grand, us sitting here discussing the future," Dad suddenly spoke up. "A few weeks ago I didn't even think I had one." His round, newly-weathered face crinkled as he beamed round at us all.

I couldn't take any more of this. I still didn't understand what had gone on between Mam and Dad. I got up. "I'm off to bed," I said. "If we go on like this we'll be turning into the Waltons."

"G'night Lyn-boy," Kev said in a phoney accent.

"G'night Kev-lass," I rejoined.

"You've got that t'wrong way round, 'aven't you?" asked Dad.

"Ladlass!"

"Lasslad!"

We both said it together. And laughed.

I waved at Mam and Dad – we don't go in for kissing goodnight – and went off upstairs. I was right about Mam's bath. There wasn't a skerrick of hot water.

Chapter 19

Roger brought the bag, the cardigan and Anna next morning.

I was a bit taken aback when she walked in ahead of him.

"Morning, Lyn. Don't worry, I'm not about to play gooseberry on your walk. Some of us have to work, you know. I need the car for my hospital shift."

"We'll drop her off as we drive to the moors," explained Roger.

"And don't, if you'll pardon the expression, go too far and forget to pick me up this afternoon." She grinned and held out the blue leather handbag. "I should have known that Bio set are a load of ageing school-kids. They were going to organise a hunt-the-handbag game later on. A variation on car-keys, I think. Fun stuff, what?"

I took the bag and opened it. "It's all here," I said. "All my best new equipment is here. Oh thanks, Anna, thanks a lot. You don't know what this means to me."

"Oh, yes I do, old cock," she smiled. "Remember me, the prospective doctor? Why, I as good as discovered your diabetes myself, that day in the shepherd's hut up on Fountains Fell." We laughed together and she sat down in Dad's chair.

Roger sat beside me. "And doesn't that seem years ago?" he asked.

"A lifetime," I agreed. "Everything's changed that much since then..."

"Nay, it's you that's changed, Lynnie Bugge," said Anna, in her vile local accent. "Tha's a diffrunt lass nowadays."

"Am I?" I was quite surprised. I knew I felt different now; but I didn't think it showed.

"Different, our lass?" asked Kev, coming in from the kitchen. "She allus was different. Ladlass we used to call her, but I see no signs now."

"I should hope not, Kevin," said Anna severely. "Who'd want to be a grotty lad when you can be a marvellous lass?"

They all laughed, and I joined in easily, without feeling at all injured. Whatever they teased me about now, I knew I could take it; I knew there are more important things than being short, wearing glasses, having ginger hair.

"Well, come on, you two." Anna got up. "I must be there before noon if I'm to put in a full shift today. God knows, I need the money if anybody's going to get any Christmas presents from me."

"Shall you give us a lift?" asked Kev. "I'm off up to the workshops to have a tour round."

"As long as you're ready right now," said Anna very firmly.

Kev leapt to attention and saluted. "Yesss maam!"

"Tell you what." I reached into Mam's bag and held up the fiver. "Treat yourselves to a taxi back and we can come home when we're ready."

"Tell you what," Roger said as we all stood up and

gathered our things. "You're a scheming little lass on the quiet, aren't you?"

We dropped the two workers off at the hospital and Roger turned the little car out to the moors. It was a bleak day and the high, open country was dun-brown under the leaden sky. There was no other colour but shades of brown and grey, with hefty splodges of black where the rocks outcropped on the fell. He parked the car where a beck slithered black amongst the tussocks.

"Featherbed Moss," he said.

I looked out at the wide, harsh scene and shuddered. His hand ruffled my hair and rested at the back of my neck. "When I think of you that night, sick and lost and alone in that terrain, I know I deserve to lose my job."

"No, you don't. You were good to me on that field course. That was the only day you weren't there to round me up from the back. It was my fault I never made friends with anybody and always walked on me own."

"Well, I don't want you to walk on your own, Lynnie Bugge. I want you to walk with me, now, often." He bent down to look into my face.

I flushed. "Well, I won't be able to do that if you're in Iceland," I said.

"No, that's true," he sighed and pulled me close. "It's going to be pretty difficult, you understand... you and me, I mean."

I nodded. I kept my eyes on Featherbed Moss and savoured the glow inside me. "I do understand," I said.

"I knew you would." And he went on to tell me of his plans. He would join the expedition in Iceland for the six months it took me to finish college. And he'd write, I'd write, even telephone sometimes.

"A settling time, a proving time. So's nobody can accuse me of spoiling your chances," he said. "Then we can take it from there. You'll be eighteen by the summer, you'll have your A-levels."

"With a lot of luck," I said.

"With a lot of hard work. That's all you need, Lyn, I know you're quite capable." He gave me a little hug. "So what's the most important thing you want to do after that?" he asked.

I thought for a moment. Nobody had ever asked me that before. To my surprise I found that I knew what I wanted. And I thought I knew what he wanted me to say I wanted.

"To write," I said. "And to be with you." I wondered whether I'd put them in the wrong order but Roger didn't seem to mind.

"You shall do both. Next summer, we'll both be at a stage where we can take a year out. I'm thinking of joining a group in Peru to survey earth-movements. If you can turn your hand to anything from cooking to writing up reports, I'm sure I can fix you a place. Your writing will grow anyway, and you might even sell some travel articles." He tipped my face round to look at him. "Will you come?" he said.

It sounded perfect. Travel, my writing and Roger. But... "I don't expect they have pen-injections in Peru," I said dolefully.

He laughed. "We can carry supplies for you – diabetics climb the Himalayas, you know. I'm not going to let you hide behind that one."

We sat in the cold little car and looked at each other. "I'm glad I'm not your teacher now, Lyn," he said.

And then he kissed me. I didn't worry about teeth clashing, breath smelling, or glasses; I kissed him back, hard. And when it was over he held my shoulders and looked right into me.

"Aach, you're a rare enough lassie," he said, and as an afterthought, "Tha knoaws."

"Aye," I said softly. "Roger, will you just promise me one thing?"

"Anything, love."

"Cut out the third-rate Yorkshire, please?"

Before he could retaliate, I shot out of the car, "Come on, then," I shouted. "Race you across Featherbed Moss."

"Lynnie . . . be careful, don't . . ." I heard him call. But I did. I missed my footing and slithered down into the beck.

"Bloody hell!" I felt the mud ooze through the lace-holes of my fell-boot. It felt familiar, soothing, even.

"Come on, Roslyn Bugge." Roger stood over me and held out a hand to pull me up. Again.

Titles in the Adlib Series

Terry Edge
Fanfare For a Teenage Warrior in Love
In two and a half extraordinary weeks at Hornford Comprehensive Tom Hall falls in love, becomes a T.V. 'personality', gets caught up in a school betting shop, plays championship football – and survives with flying colours.
0 233 98080 6

Double-Crossing Duo
Further adventures of Tom Hall and Taff, now two years older and living in Wales, but still full of schemes and ideas.   0 233 98319 8

Will Gatti
Berry Moon
An old family feud explodes into violence in the west of Ireland.   0 233 97828 3

Dennis Hamley
Blood Line
A long standing family feud depicted in a television drama series fuses with Rory's real life and forces him to act to save his mother from being the last victim in the chain.
0 233 98445 3

Coded Signals
A short story collection featuring tales of the unusual, unexpected and unexplained.   0 233 98541 7

Charles Hannam
A Boy in Your Situation
A remarkable autobiography which follows the experiences of a young Jewish boy who flees to England as a refugee from Nazi Germany.   0 233 98279 5

Minfong Ho
Rice Without Rain
Famine in a Thai village make an insecure background for Ned and Jinda's uneasy romance.   0 233 97911 5

James Jauncey
The Albatross Conspiracy
Christine and Tom's plan to thwart a gang of violent terrorists bent on blowing up a Nato fuel base in southern Scotland involved them in kidnap, and could have ended in their deaths.   0 233 98585 9

Rhodri Jones
Different Friends
It was learning the truth about Azhar that shocked Chris into changing his attitude to love, making him think for the first time what the word really meant.   0 233 98096 2

Hillsden Riots and Getting It Wrong
Two of Rhodri Jones' most powerful novels reprinted in one volume. Both are concerned with the problems confronting black teenagers in urban Britain.   0 233 98708 8

Slaves and Captains
A version of Herman Melville's *Benito Cereno*, the true story of an 18th century slave ship and the strange events that occur on it.   0 233 98356 2

Them and Us
This is a collection of tough short stories about young lives, shaped by neglect, misunderstanding, prejudice and, sometimes, friendship.   0 233 98709 6

Pete Johnson
Catch You On the Flip Side
A sharp, lighthearted look at what happens to a boy, accustomed to girls falling for him, when he falls in love himself.   0 233 98074 1

Geraldine Kaye
A Piece of Cake
In this second Amy story, a sequel to *A Breath of Fresh Air*, Geraldine Kaye skilfully weaves the threads of the old slave life in Jamaica with modern Amy's Bristol life.
0 233 98712 6

Great Comfort
Comfort Kwatey Jones is half British and half Ghanaian. She loves being in Ghana, but when she goes to stay with her grandmother there, she discovers that she does not know the country and its traditions as well as she imagines.
0 233 98300 7

Someone Else's Baby
Partly because of her conventional family Terry tries to ignore the fact that she is pregnant, but the birth of her baby completely changes her life.   0 233 98575 1

John Kirkbride
In Reply to Your Advertisement
Kevin Daughtry may not have a job but he is a persistent and imaginative letter writer and through his application letters and the replies he receives we get to know him more and like him better.   0 233 98344 9

Thank You For Your Application
Kevin Daughtry, once an unemployment statistic, now has a job and ambitions to write. Efforts to be 'great' result in rejections, but a more popular style seems likely to win through.   0 233 98446 1

Sorry, Not Quite
Inspired by the acceptance of one story Kevin Daughtry soldiers on, in spite of withering rejection letters. Perseverance wins, and fortune once again smiles as Kevin refuses to take 'no' for an answer.   0 233 98717 7

Elisabeth Mace
Under Seige
The fantasy world of a sophisticated board game become an obession with Morris Nelson and the characters involved in the game more important than the people around him.
0 233 98345 7

Beware the Edge
The perils of dabbling in the supernatural.   0 233 97908 5

Sue Mayfield
I Carried You on Eagle's Wings
For Tony caring for an injured seagull was especially important because he felt so inadequate about helping his mother, who was dying of multiple sclerosis.   0 233 98576 X

Suzanne Newton
I Will Call It Georgie's Blues
Bitter family tension threatens the youngest son of a preacher in the American Deep South.   0 233 97720 1

Bette Paul
Ladlass
When Lyn collapsed with diabetes on a field study weekend, her life changed dramatically. She not only became the reluctant focal point of student and family politics, but fell in love.   0 233 98710 X

Eduardo Quiroga
On Foreign Ground
A young Argentinian soldier in the Falklands remembers his love affair with an English girl.   0 233 97909 3

Lorna Read
The Lies They Tell
Ann is an ordinary teenager until a blow to the head leaves her with thought-reading powers and the knowledge that a prospective candidate is lying to the electorate. Proving it turns her into a temporary celebrity.   0 233 98444 5

Caryl Rivers
Virgins
A bitter-sweet story of American high school girls growing up in the fifties.   0 233 97791 0

Malcolm Rose
The Highest Form of Killing
A chilling tale, starting with a tragedy on a Devon beach and ending in horrific tension, which highlights the dangers of manufacturing toxins for chemical warfare.   0 233 98589 1

Son of Pete Flude
Seb, son of pop-idol Pete Flude, is cheerful by nature and no fool. Both qualities help him survive an evil kidnap by drug dealers seeking to counter an undercover police operation.   0 233 98711 8

Michael Rosen
The Deadman Tapes
Paul Deadman's curiosity is aroused by eight remarkable tapes, apparently the confessions and life stories of a group of young people. Who are these people? Where are they now? Did they know each other? Who made the tapes?
0 233 98443 7

Andy Tricker
Accidents Will Happen
The author's own moving account of a motorbike accident which left him paralysed, and his struggle to regain a measure of independence.   0 233 98095 4

Rosemary Wells
The Man in the Woods
Is he an ordinary hooligan or a more sinister figure mysteriously connected with events of the American Civil War of a hundred years ago?   0 233 97785 6